THE GRIND

AN URBAN TALE OF HONOR AND DECEPTION

BRAVO "DRE" MARENTZ

PublishAmerica
Baltimore

First printing

All characters in this book are fictitious, and any resemblance to real persons, living or dead, is coincidental.

ISBN: 1-60610-209-5
PUBLISHED BY PUBLISHAMERICA, LLLP
www.publishamerica.com
Baltimore

Printed in the United States of America

I dedicate this book to my wife and children, Thank you for believing in me when no one else did.

I would also like to thank the Goodin family. Without them, I would have never found out what it meant to be alone.

Last but not least, the Bills family, I love every one of you.

Lyfe? What kind of fucked-up name was that for a man to have? I may not have liked his name at first, but his music really hits home for me. As I sit here listening to his music, I couldn't help but wonder how I got here.

I have been living this lifestyle for a long time now. I couldn't blame others for the mistakes I'd made. I also know that we all have a beginning, and it was up to us where we end. All I could do was wonder, was this the end for me?

I should just take you back to the beginning, and maybe then, not only would you know how I started, but it might just help you see how I got where I am now.

CHAPTER ONE

I was born in St. Louis, Missouri, to a mother that was too young to have me, and to a father that was too cool to want me. As a child my mother was all I needed and she was all I got. I am not saying that she did not do her best, let me just say...things did get a li'l hard from time to time.

That was the beginning of the most intense training you could ever have. All these years I have heard people mention street knowledge, but until you have it, you couldn't understand it.

I find it funny that, even though I have hundreds of memories from my childhood most of them are bad, yet I couldn't figure out just which one put me on this pathway. I think the first one that came to mind was my mother's then boyfriend, ripping the phone out of the wall and throwing it out of the window as she and I ran from the apartment, she dragging me behind her.

I can also remember as a li'l boy, going to the neighborhood bar to see if I could find the weed man, Leo, to get weed for my mom, damn those were some fat bags. Yet, for some reason my mother to this day, told me it never happened. But she can't explain how I knew Leo sold weed.

Then there was the time my uncle had me come help him pull these huge sticky plants out of the ground and take them to his basement in big black bags, I wasn't even ten years old yet. I did not know what they were then but I do remember thinking that they really looked funny hanging from the ceiling and they had a funny smell.

I can even remember my older cousin Juan teaching me how to roll these really cool looking cigarettes that we smoked. Wow that was a real funny feeling, I felt so good. All I ever wanted was to feel that good every day for the rest of my life.

The most violent memory was the day I found my uncle dead on his living room floor with the back of his head bloody as hell. A so-called girlfriend and a few of her friends killed him. Can you believe that bitch killed my uncle over a li'l funky-ass gold phone and a few dollars? He always taught me to treat other people good, and they would do the same for you. That was hard on me; I damn near went crazy, but it was not what got to me most.

Out of all the hurtful things I remember, out of all the hard times I thought I had, nothing bothered me more than the day my mother told me, "You should be more like the Shepards' kids." All I wanted from my mother was love. I wanted her to love me for me.

To all those of you who are parents, listen to me now: never compare your kids to others in a negative way, you could end up sending them down the wrong path, or even worse, they could end up hating you. I knew when she said that, she had no clue that the Shepards' daughter was already sexing me up, and smoking more weed than I was. I guess that's what happens when kids get together in church. Not long after that, we moved to Baltimore, Maryland. There, we could get a fresh start.

I really loved my mother, all I wanted was for her to be proud of me. However, I am sure you can already guess, it never happened, and from the looks of things, it never would.

Even as an adult, trying to turn my life around, I could not do anything right as far as my mother was concerned, not even raise my kids. Can you believe that I even had to hear, from my li'l 10-year-old sister how my mother told her all I did was mess up, and how I couldn't do anything right?

You know what, if that was how she wanted it, if that was what everyone wanted from me, I was going to show the world how bad I can be. I'll just go back to my roots and do what I do best. Back to the beginning, but of what, no one knew but everyone soon would.

Let me tell you how one of the most tender and loving li'l boys you could have ever met, became such a feared and respected drug dealer.

Like I said before, I loved my mother, and I don't know if she loved me, but she had a bad habit of comparing me to those that she thought were so much better than I was. Moreover, with each comparison, every time I heard "You should be more like..." another layer of darkness and hatred formed.

I knew the children that she respected and admired so much, and I knew them well. What my mother did not realize was, these kids that she wanted me to be like, were doing everything that she claimed she did not want me to do.

You see, what she didn't know about was the smoking, the drinking, the drugs, and the sex that was going on right up under her nose, and as bad as she thought I was, I hadn't yet become a major part of their world. She wanted me to be more like them, so that's what I set out to do. However, I did not want to be just like them, I was determined to be better than they were at their own game, so that's what I was going to do.

As hard as I tried, I was never good at being a follower, so merely being a part of this so-called group was not good enough for me, I had to be number one, I had to run shit. As far as I was concerned, these fools had weak minds and I was going to use that to my advantage. Within a couple of months I had each and every one of them coming to me for everything: drugs, liquor, the girls came for sex, you name it.

Not only did I become their supplier, but I also had them doing anything they could to keep me happy. Hell, I had become a parent's worst nightmare. The boys were stealing and selling drugs for me, and the girls were fucking and sucking me whenever I had the slightest thought about sex.

That year I decided I was through trying to make my mother happy. It was time for me to think about me, it was time for me to be happy with me, and the one thing that I learned made me happy was power.

I had spent most of my life trying to make others happy without being happy myself. I was going to be happy if it was the last thing I did.

I never wanted to be the bad guy, I just wanted people to accept me as I was. I tried to do everything right, no matter how it made me feel. All I really cared about was seeing everyone around me smiling, and somehow part of me still feels that way. Who would have ever imagined, a thug with a heart.

My mother had remarried a guy that wanted to be the boss of my home, so it was time for me to go somewhere that I could be the boss. I wasn't the type to stay there, living in another man's house, so I got out and lived off the one thing that I thought loved me, I lived off the streets. From that point on, I made sure that whatever person I encountered, wanted to be around me, wanted to be like me. I needed a fresh start; it was time for me to make a fresh start...a fresh start back in St. Louis.

I returned to my roots, a place where I could be free. It's on now, here I come world, and I hope you're ready. It was hard at first, but after a few bumps and bruises, I was working my way to the top.

I had nothing but my conversation skills and wit, so that's what I used to get back on my feet. Shit, in no time I had dealers in the hood begging me to work for them, so that's what I did, to start anyway. I was hungry though, fuck it, I wasn't hungry I was greedy. I had the customers, I had the connects, fuck this shit, I didn't want to be a worker...I wanted to be the boss.

I started down a road that I knew I would never be able to come back up. I began to build my "business" my "organization." It took me about 6 months, and somehow I ended up with 10 of the most evil, ruthless, as far as I knew, loyal, mother-fuckers you could ask for.

So there we were, all hungry, young, and ready. We began to slowly eliminate anyone that we thought could ever be a threat to us. However, we did it in a way that even the smartest nigga in the streets couldn't figure out who was doing it.

It's sad but one of a hustler's biggest weakness was greed, if not for material shit, the opposite sex. Being from the streets my crew had no problem finding a few "rock stars" to clean up and turn on to a few of the "big boys." Those dumb-ass niggas, thinking with their dicks, a lot of good that did them when they found out that they were HIV positive. If we could not get rid of them that way, we had no problem taking them out and dumping their asses in a river somewhere. Those fuckers started running away like dogs with their tails between their legs.

I know I destroyed many lives and many families, but I didn't make them lay down with women they didn't even know, and I didn't make them get in the game. Hell, they did not care about us, we wanted to eat too, what about our families. Actually, they often called us, "the young, dumb niggas."

They may have thought we were dumb, but it took us less than two years to take over the city. We supplied everything to everybody. The city was ours at last. Who would have thought that things could ever fall apart? Not us, not the crew, that could never happen. I told you what a hustler's biggest weakness was...maybe you forgot that we were hustlers too.

CHAPTER TWO

Music played loudly as an old black Chevy Nova pulls up to a crowd of teenagers standing on the corner of Garfield and Vander Venter Ave. The tinted window slowly lowered. "What's up, fools?" I said aloud to the young niggas standing there.

High-Top was the youngest member of this crew. He was a tall slim motherfucker with one of those crazy ass haircuts. He wasn't the toughest member of the crew but he was just as hungry as the rest of us. High-Top walked up to the car with the craziest grin on his face and passed me two paper bags. One was a bottle of M.D. 20/20. The other was a bag of money.

"We have a problem," he told me.

"What's that?" I said as I took a sip of wine.

"There's a new crew trying to move in on our shit, Dre," he said, no longer smiling.

"Stop bullshitin' man; that's not even funny," I responded. I knew he wasn't joking; one thing he never fucked around about was business.

"Who are they, and where are they from?" I asked him.

"I'm working on that info for you now," he said as I passed the bottle back to him.

I told him, "Set up a meeting for in the morning. Make it at the yard, and tell everyone to be there."

The yard, this was a spot you would never even think about if you were a cop; it really was just a yard though. It was a vacant lot that my grandfather owned with a 10-foot fence all the way around it. In the middle was a shack that we had built out of old lumber. It wasn't huge, but it was big enough for about 15 people to sit in and play dominoes. It was our spot to hang out. We could see every inch of the lot around us, and we had a fire barrel just in case we needed to dump shit real quick.

As far as being robbed, we had our guns but never really cared about being caught with them. I was taught it was always better to be caught alive with your gun, than dead without it.

Reggie was my driver. He was a couple of years older than the rest of us but we all thought he was cool, so we felt he would be a great addition to our crew. Not to mention the fact he was one of the best drivers that any of us had ever seen.

"What do you think about that?" Reggie asked me as we drove away.

I heard what he said, but I said nothing right away. I really couldn't believe that some one thought that they could move in on us like that. Who was brave enough to do some dumb shit like that?

"I really don't know what to think," I said after a long while, "but I do know that we're going to send these fools a message. I'm sick of this shit."

"Yeah, I know how you feel," he responded.

"Let's go get Phil," I said, and I ended the conversation.

Phil, had known me the longest. Our mothers had been good friends for years, and neither of them had a clue about what we were doing or they just didn't care. He was the ladies' man, with his long Jerry curl, and he had a proper way of talking. I remember the way it pissed me off to always hear the girls say, "I love the way you talk. It's so proper."

I hated it. Phil loved it. I knew it was just jealousy.

He lived in a li'l spot not too far away on Labadie Avenue. Whenever there was a problem, I would talk it out with Phil. Between the two of us, we could come up with the solution to anything.

"Blow the horn." I don't know why I had to tell Reggie this, but I did. He gave the horn a few taps, and after about 10 minutes Phil came to the door.

"What's up, Dre?" he yelled.

"Let's go. We got work to do," was all I had to say. Phil and I had decided a long time ago all we did was have fun, so if I said it was, "work," it had to be something bad.

After a few minutes, Phil came out and to my surprise; he had my number-one nigga with him, "Hot-Rod." Now this motherfucker was the realist nigga out of all of them. Even though we had only known each other a couple years, we had grown to be closer than brothers. We had our problems, and I knew he did not forgive me for all the shit I got him caught up in, but he was still down and ready for whatever. All I could do is think, *That's my nigga,* and I was happy as hell to see him.

"Where the weed at?" The first thing out of Hot-Rod's mouth every time I saw him.

"In your pocket, where it always is." The same thing I normally said, so nothing was different about this time.

We all laughed as they got into the back seat.

However, the laughter ended as I told them the news I had just heard from High-Top.

"So what do you want to do about it?" came from the back seat with a grumble.

"The same thing we always do," I said as I turned to look at the men in the back seat. "We're going to get rid of them."

They all knew exactly what I was saying. It wasn't the first time, and it damn sure was not going to be the last time we made someone disappear. Part of me knew that all of them loved this part of the business, and not so deep inside I loved it too.

"Let's go get something to eat," I said, then turned the radio up and we headed to Ms. Collins, the best soul-food restaurant in the Lou.

Even though the music was loud as shit, the car seemed to be quiet as hell. Every one of us was deep into thought, we all had our own way of taking care of shit, but one thing we had in common, we were all thinkers. It was almost funny just how quite we were. We were normally loud and laughing; to shut us up, just mention trouble. However, the silence would not last long; it would end a lot sooner than any of us would have imagined.

We hadn't made it but a few blocks when Reggie noticed that red Caddie following us.

"What the fuck is this?" he said almost in a whisper.

"Yeah, I see it, too," said Hot-Rod, as he pulled out a chrome .45 auto he had bought just a couple days before.

Phil looked at him. "Looks like you're going to get to use that thing a lot sooner than you thought, nigga."

I looked at Reggie. "You got your shit?"

He looked at me and shook his head, no.

"Can you make it back to High-Top?" I asked.

His response was the one I always heard from him. "I can make it to the moon if you need me to."

Reggie picked up his speed a li'l, and so did the Caddie, but they didn't try anything, not yet any way. As we pulled up on the block, High-Top could see that something was not right; I could see him pulling out that brand-new .357 that I had just given him not even a month before, for his 19th birthday. We pulled up and got out of the car. Just as Reggie rounded the front of the car, Ant, one of High-Top's workers threw him a gun. It seemed as soon as the gun hit Reggie's hands, the Caddie windows started to lower, and I could see the barrel of at least one shotgun sticking out.

I heard, "Look out!" Just then, shots rang out,

both from the Caddie and from us. It sounded like a war had just broke out on that small street corner, and we were all right in the middle of it. I could hear bullets buzzing past my ears every time I rose up and took a shot. It looked as if we were getting the upper hand in this fight as the Caddie ran into the curb and the last two men that were in the car got out of the car blasting at us.

"Shoot those mother fuckers!" was the last thing I heard Ant yell. Just then another car, I'm not sure just what kind it was, came up from the other direction and all of a sudden, there were six more mother fuckers behind us shooting, too.

I was never really that close to Ant, but when I saw his head explode from the bullet that entered it, it seemed to anger me even more. He was a young handheld that never really listened to anything you told him, but he would do damn near anything to show his loyalty.

I rose up my two blue steel .45s and started to fire. As I fired to the left, I saw my bullets strike a short, stocky dude; somehow I couldn't help but think he looked familiar to me. I fired three more shots to the right and hit a tall white guy that I had never seen before. Hot-Rod fired over my shoulder into one of the people that got out of the back seat of the second car. He fell to the ground and screamed out in pain.

"There's one more, behind you!" I yell out to Phil. He turned and fired three shots into the last asshole, and we watched as his chest exploded. A mist of blood filled the air as he fell to the ground.

"Is that all of them?" Reggie asked.

"It looks like it," I tell him.

"Let's get the fuck out of here!" I ran and jumped in the car. "High-Top, get everybody the fuck out of here!" I yelled to him, "Meet us at Gino's crib!"

We sped off and just as we get a few blocks away, the fucking police pull behind us.

"What kind of shit is this? Reggie, get us the fuck out of here, fast!" I didn't mean to yell at him, but I was pumped, it had been a long time since we had a good shootout.

We were speeding out west on Martin Luther King drive when Hot-Rod noticed police coming right at us. Phil was not happy about it.

"We might have to shoot our way out of it, niggas." None of us wanted to admit it, but we knew he was right.

"Sometimes you got to do what you got to do." I don't know why but it seems like every time some shit was going down Hot-Rod said the same shit.

I had to hope for the best. "What do you think, Regg?"

In a calm cool voice he replied, "I'll do my best; we just have to wait and see."

"Oh, shit!" Phil yelled out from the back seat.

Then Hot-Rod yelled out, "Road block dead ahead!"

The tires squealed as Reggie slammed on the breaks as he tried to make a hard left turn.

Reggie yelled, "Hold on, guys! I don't think we're going to make it!"

Just as he finished his sentence Phil shouts, "FUCK, LOOK OUT!"

All we could see was that brick wall coming at us so fast, it seemed to be moving in slow motion.

CHAPTER THREE

The blue suburban sped down highway 70 headed toward St. Louis with two crazy niggas in it. Alpo, the driver was a short light skin motherfucker with green eyes and short wavy hair. He wasn't a bad person but he often had problems with the women and his temper. Alpo's biggest problem was that he wanted the money and he wanted it now, he was a great rapper but it was not paying him good enough, so he turned to a life of drug smuggling.

If I could have helped Alpo out of the game, I wouldn't have, cause the money was too fast and we paid him well. He was a loyal motherfucker though. Bake was the second one in the truck, he wasn't the brightest crayon in the box, and actually, he was more like the chalk in the crayon box. None of us really knew a lot about Bake, he just started hanging out with Alpo and his boys and some kind of way they ended up friends.

"Your ass needs to learn how to drive, Bake," Alpo said.

"I, I, I, I, I do know how to drive; you just don't let, let, let me."

"That's because we need to make it to St. Louis with this shit for Dre," Alpo said with a laugh. "If I let you drive we'll fuck around and end up in Texas."

Bake looked at Alpo as if his feelings were hurt. "That's fucked u, u, u, up, man."

"Maybe, but it's true," Alpo said to Bake with a smirk then turned his attention back to the highway after seeing a sign saying, "St. Louis 91 miles."

"Yo, Bake, don't cry like a li'l bitch. We'll be there in a couple hours, then we'll see if we can find a bitch dumb enough to give you some pussy," Alpo said to his friend, who just sat there and stared out the window as if he were deep in thought.

There was nothing else said the rest of the trip, or at least until they crossed the river into St. Louis.

"I just love seeing the Arch," was the first thing Bake said in almost two hours.

"Shit. I thought you were dead over there, acting like a li'l bitch," Alpo said, looking at Bake as if he hated him.

"Wh, wh, wh, where are we going this time?"

"You don't need to know, but we're going to Lott's house this time." Then Alpo turned and looked at Bake. "Why, you going to have the feds meet us there?"

Again Bake looked down and came back with the same thing he always said when Alpo got to him. "F, f, f, fuck you."

Lott was the oldest member of our group; he was a family man, with two families. Lott was a true playa; he had his wife and kids living on one side of town, and his girlfriend and her kids on the other side of town. I never knew why Lott didn't just pick one or the other, but if they liked it, I loved it. He had been in the game for many years, so we all looked up to him, but truth be known, even though we asked for his advice we never really listened to it.

"Niecy, they'll be here soon, so I want you to take the kids out for a while," Lott said to his girlfriend. He was smart never to have his family around when he was dealing with drugs.

"Okay," she said, "but I need some money."

"You always need money; you're as bad as my wife." He knew as soon as it left his mouth that he had said the wrong thing, but for some reason she said nothing, nothing at all. He would pay for this mistake later; he just didn't know when, and he didn't know how.

Just as Niecy was leaving, Mike and Tank drove up in a clean-ass '68 Chevy, all white inside and out. These where the two biggest mother fuckers I had ever seen in my life, between the two of them you're looking at over 600 pounds of muscle, both of them standing over 6 feet 7 inches. These two guys were the so-called enforcers of our group. When they went out to collect from someone, they got what they went for.

Mike and Tank were the last two members of our group, but at times, you would think they were the group themselves. Their biggest problem was the fact that they were too well known, and it wasn't their fault; they just could not be missed. Wherever they happened to be everyone took notice of them.

"What's up, Niecy?" Mike barked out with a voice as deep as the Mississippi river itself.

"He's in the house," she said without as much as a hello.

Tank never bothered to speak to Niecy; he always said it was because she made him nervous. Can you imagine a nigga as big as him nervous around anyone? I couldn't, and the thought of it always made me laugh. They continued to walk to the house, as Niecy and the kids got in her car and drove off.

"Damn, there's a lot of police down that street. Let's get the fuck out of here!" Alpo always seemed to see the police; I guess that's why he made such a good smuggler.

"W, w, w, w, what do you think they're doing down there?" Bake said, sounding like a li'l kid.

"Don't know, and I don't care," Alpo said in response.

Alpo drove on, making sure to keep his speed under control, that would have been some crazy shit, being busted just a few blocks from your final stop. They saw several police cars driving around the neighborhood, so it was as if they were driving on thin ice. After about 15 minutes, they made it to Lott's house. As they drove up both guys finally felt safe, or at least they felt better.

"I think they're here," Tank said as he stood up, grabbed his 12-gauge, and walked to the back door.

"Is it them?" Mike asked.

From the back room, you could hardly hear Lott. "It better be!" Soon after he came out dressed in a pair of old, torn jeans and a dusty, blue tee shirt. You would have never thought that this motherfucker was a major drug dealer, but maybe that's how he stayed under the cops' radar so long, by dressing, "third class," as we called it. He barked out orders. "Mike, get up top and take a look around. I heard a lot of cops out there not too long ago; I don't want anything to go wrong. Tank, keep an eye out that door. If it even looks like someone is trying to come in, blast them fools."

Tank asked, "Do you think them dumb asses know to stay in the truck this time?"

"They better know," Lott said, "but if not, their fault."

Alpo backs onto the parking pad behind Lott's house and turned off the engine. "Now all we need to do is wait on the all clear," he said looking at Bake.

"Th, th, th, they n, n, need to hurry u, u, up bef, fo, fo, before it gets hot o, o, o, out here."

"Damn fool, you sound like a fucking scratched record; you need to go see a doctor or something about that shit," Alpo said with a laugh.

Even though he often teased Bake about his speech, deep inside he felt a li'l sorry for him. That I believed was the reason that he insisted on Bake being a part of the organization. He took care of that nigga as if he was his child or something.

"All clear!" Mike shouted down from up top.

Lott had built what you could call a watchtower,

at the top of his house just for days like this. It wasn't very high but the ceiling was high enough for Mike to fit his tall ass up there.

It was reinforced with steel and concrete walls, floors, and ceilings. I don't know how but that fucker even had four or five gun cabinets up there. Even though we never had to, I think we could have fit 20 people up there with food and guns. Now that I think about it, he really had a bunker on top of his house.

Hell, you could have blown the house up, and the only thing that would have made it through the explosion would have been that room.

"All right, Tank, bring 'em in," Lott barked out. Tank headed out the back door to the truck.

"Yo, here comes Tank," Alpo mumbled to Bake.

Tank walked up to the driver's side. "What's up, niggas? Let's go."

Bake and Alpo got out of the truck, and all three of them walked around to the back of it. Alpo opened the back and each man grabbed two of the six military style duffle bags that were there, and went into the house.

"What's up L, L, L, Lott?" Bake said almost too low to hear.

"What's up, Elvis?" Lott responded.

"Three hundred pounds," Tank told Lott.

"And it looks like some good shit," Alpo added.

Lott looked at Alpo. "I thought it was only going to be 200 this week."

"We just follow orders. Dre told us what to pick up, and that's what we did," Alpo said.

"That's right, fools; you don't want me to come deal with you," Tank said as if he was joking, but they all knew it was true.

"Did you see all those c, c, c, c, cops out there?" Bake asked Lott.

"I saw a lot of them out there, but I don't know what the hell they're doing. Let's get this shit weighed and put up; I'll have Mike hook up the scanner and see if he can find out anything." Lott was concerned but not worried.

Without being told, Tank bought the scales in and set them up on the dining room table, then turned and went to tell Mike about the scanner.

Mike never minded being up top, as a matter of fact I think he liked it. Often he would go up top to just sit back, chill out and smoke a fat one. The rest of us did not really like it much, not because it was small or anything, but because when you were up there it seemed like we were preparing for war or something. We all wanted to believe we were ready for whatever, but we didn't ever want to get to the point that we needed the room. That's why we did whatever we could to avoid the police whenever possible.

Lott could weigh, bag, and wrap about 300 pounds in a li'l less than an hour. He hadn't thought much about the police outside or anything else, when he was taking care of business he was usually like that.

Alpo and Bake had struck up a game of two hand spades in the corner. Tank sat at the table and wrapped everything after Lott weighed and bagged everything. Everything was going smooth, and then Lott decided that he wanted to know if Mike had heard anything on the scanner.

"Hey, dumb ass, go up and see if Mike heard anything about the police yet," he yelled at Alpo.

"Yes, sir," Alpo said, trying to be funny. Lott just looked at him as he walked away to go up top.

Mike was just listening to some police chatter when Alpo poked his head up through the hatch. Before Alpo could get anything out of his mouth, Mike yelled, "GET LOTT NOW!" Mike heard something that seemed to upset him on the scanner, and he needed to tell Lott fast.

"What's up, Mike?" Lott said before he even made it all the way up top.

"It sounds like Dre and Reggie are in trouble," he responded. "They're chasing a black Chevy Nova, and it sounds like the chase started over by the yard."

"Oh, shit, what happened?" Lott asked.

All Mike could say was the one thing that Lott did not want to hear, "I don't know." Not only did he not want to tell him that, he really didn't want to say it either.

Lott went back down stairs and started to put everything away. Of course, he was worried about Dre but he knew he had to clean up before he could do anything to help. He could hardly think right knowing that Dre was in trouble. He sent Alpo and Bake outside to keep an eye out, he didn't know why Dre was in trouble, and he was not sure if the trouble was coming his way. He felt like it was better to be safe than sorry.

It took about 30 minutes to get the house cleaned, soon as they finished, they were ready to get out in the streets. Lott called Gino to see if he heard anything from Dre.

"Did you hear the news?" he asked Gino.

"I heard, and I think they're on their way here," Gino said.

"Why, what's up?" Lott wanted to know.

"High-Top called and told me they were headed this way when they left the corner," Gino told him. "He told me they had a problem on the corner right before all this shit happened."

"Fuck...how bad was it?"

"Ant went down for good. And he did tell me the problem wasn't solved yet, either."

"I'll be there shortly; put everybody on point. Dre can make it there; Reggie's the best driver there is."

Shit was bad, and nobody knew just how bad things were going to get. Everyone was worried, but knew they had to keep their cool.

Lott told everyone, "Grab your shit, and let's go." Tank, Alpo, and Bake rode together, and Mike rode with Lott. Within minutes they were on their way.

Gino was one of my go-to guys for a few years now. He was Hot-Rod's cousin and he took care of shit on the south side of town. He was a big guy but because of his joking nature, many people got the impression that he was a soft nigga. He would laugh and play almost all the time but if you pissed him off, it was like being trapped in a cage with a hungry lion. Nobody really respected Gino as much as they should have, but they knew if they ever did anything but show him respect, no matter how they felt about him, they would have to deal with me.

Even though I cared about everyone in my crew, Hot-Rod, Gino, and Phil were the ones that I really considered my brothers, they were the closest out of everybody.

Gino was mad as hell but he remained in control, he knew that was the only way he would be able to help. He made sure everyone knew what was going on and ready for anything that might happen.

CHAPTER FOUR

"What's going on with the job I sent Donald Dims to do?" Ericka asked Manny, her right-hand man in crime.

"I don't know; I haven't heard from him yet," he said to her in his squeaky voice.

"Well, I think you need to fuckin' find out, and find out now," she said, sounding very upset.

Ericka was not the finest woman in the world, but she was definitely about making money. She would do anything and everything to get what she wanted, and I mean *anything*. I wouldn't say she was a hoe; well, then again, she was a hoe in every meaning of the word.

By the time she was 18 years old, she had gone through more men than the Army. I'm not sure why she started fucking every man she could or where she learned the business, but I do know that she learned it well. In as little as 1 year from the time she started hustling, she had put together the only crew that would ever give me and my crew a problem.

"Damn!" Ericka exclaimed, "I need to know what the fuck is going on. Did Donald get the job done or what?"

Manny came into the room. "I think he fucked up."

"Why do you say that?" she responded.

He picked up the television remote and turned on the TV. The TV was barely on when they heard the reporters on the scene of a bloody shootout say, "...several people are dead." One of the only names they recognized right away was that of Donald; he was the one who was supposed to be getting the job done.

They never said any names from my crew, so they knew things did not go their way. Shit wasn't looking good for them, and they knew it, but they didn't know if any of my top members were taken out.

Ericka was pissed as hell, and Manny knew it. Sometimes the best thing to do when she was upset was to stay the fuck out of her way, but he never had enough sense to do it.

"Hey, baby," he mumbled, "let's go fuck."

"Is that all you ever think about?" she barked.

He tried to sound as caring as possible. "But baby, I'm horny."

He only seemed to anger her more, to the point that she was in tears and yelling. "I wouldn't let you lick the crack of my ass right now, so just shut the fuck up talking to me before I send your ass out there to get shot."

He really wanted to respond, but for the first time since he met her, he knew that she meant what she said, and he remained silent as he exited the room.

Ericka was upset, but she never felt defeated. She was determined to take out my crew and she thought she knew how to do it. She never said why she hated me so much and I never knew why. I couldn't understand what I did to her to make her feel that way about me, truth be known I didn't care. I had known her for years and never did anything against her. At one time, I even considered her a friend, that's why I never would have thought she was trying to take me out.

Ericka spent the next few hours trying to regroup for her next attack on me. She called Lee, another one of her flunkies that tried to be tough but he was really just a li'l bitch, then she called her white boy Matt. Matt gave new meaning to the word, "Wigger;"

he tried so hard to be black that most people spent their time laughing at him instead of listening to him.

When these two guys got together it was like being at a fucking comedy show after smoking' some good weed, you were guaranteed to laugh. Ericka didn't have much of a choice though, between Manny, Lee, and Matt, the only thing they had going for them was the fact that no one would ever think they were guilty of anything but being stupid.

By the time Matt and Lee arrived at Ericka's East St. Louis loft, things had calmed down quite a bit, but you could tell she was still pissed.

"I'm sick of that fucker always getting away," she said in a soft shaky voice. "Every time we get close to finishing him off he gets away."

"So what do you want us to do?" Matt said, trying to put as much bass in his voice as possible.

She paced back and forth a few minutes. "We need to get an inside man."

"Or woman." Manny squeaked out. Everyone knew he had a one-track mind, and he never tried to hide it.

"Do you have anybody in mind?" Lee said while scratching himself.

Ericka thought for a second. "Manny might just be right about using a woman." She knew how it sounded, Manny right about something. That never happened. "If we can get one of his buddies to fall for a bitch that's loyal to me, she might just be able to get close enough to take Dre out."

The four of them nodded in agreement and began to work out their plan.

Shantae was a good friend of Ericka's, and they were about on the same level when it came to using their pussies as a weapon. She was about 5 feet of fire, in more than one way. She burned up more men than napalm did in Vietnam. She wasn't ugly at all, but she got men not with her looks, but because she was just that big of a freak. She didn't care who you were, as long as you had some weed to smoke, you could have her. She was willing to do anything it took to get high; it was as if she was hooked on crack.

Ericka called Shantae up and had her come by the loft. When she got there, she was ready for whatever. Anything bad and Shantae wanted in, but she didn't realize just how far she would have to go this time, this might just be her last job if she wasn't careful.

"This has to work," Ericka said with a hint of

desperation. "I don't know what else to try. Fuck, I just hate him so much."

"Why?" Shantae asked.

"I just do." She had her reasons, and for now, they would remain a secret.

Lee and Matt sat on the sofa watching TV as the other three worked out the details of their master plan. It was as if they were in church talking during the sermon. All you could hear for hours was the whisperings of three desperate people.

Every once in a while you could hear laughter among them, sometimes you could even hear things starting to heat up among them. They plotted and planned well into the night, so long, that by the time they finished, the sun had come up and shone in on Matt and Lee, asleep on the couch the next morning.

"Shantae, don't fuck up," Ericka begged of her. She had faith in her, but she also knew that Shantae sometimes was too emotionally attached. Sometimes she actually seemed to catch feelings for her victims. In addition, this time that she could not afford it. Therefore, Erika wanted to make sure that Shantae could stay in control, because if not, their plan would never work.

CHAPTER FIVE

"Oh, shit!" was all I could seem to get out of my mouth as we came inches from the brick wall. As soon, he could straighten out the car Reggie stomped on the gas and took off. As I looked in the rear view, I could see one of the police cars that was chasing us crashing into the wall.

Before another police car could get behind us, Reggie turned down an alley and pulled into an old abandoned garage. Everyone got out of the car and prepared to shoot our way out, but we didn't have to. We could hear the sirens flying up and down the streets around us, and the ghetto bird flying over us, but for some reason not one police car came down the alley.

"Damn, man, that was some driving!" Hot-Rod said with a sigh of relief.

All Reggie could say was, "Yeah, I know."

Everyone laughed in agreement. We decided to lay low for a while and wait for things to cool down.

"I think I'm going to try to get to a phone and call Gino and let him know where we are so he can come get us," Phil said with a hint of nervousness in his voice.

I simply told him, "Be careful."

Nothing else needed to be said. He slowly and carefully left the garage and walked down the alley. I watched Phil as he arrived at the end of the alley and turned left, going to what I hope was the nearest phone. You may wonder why we didn't just use our cell phones, it was one of our rules that if anything happened with the police, cut them off in case they were tracking them. The funny thing was we spent so much money on our phones, and the one time we needed them the most, we didn't use them.

"Damn, I hope he makes it," said Reggie.

I felt just as nervous as the others did. "He'll make it."

"I hope Gino's at home," said Hot-Rod.

We all knew how Gino was; he rarely stayed at home this time of day, and there was no way Phil was going to call his cell, no matter how bad things got.

"He'll be there," I told them.

We watched out for any police, and even though we saw them passing by the end of the alley, for some reason they never came our way. The phone only rang one time before Gino picked it up.

"Hello," he said.

"Gino, this is Phil. We need you, and we need you now."

Though his heart was pounding, Gino asked, "Is anyone hurt?" mostly concerned about Hot-Rod and me.

"Everyone's okay for now, but the police are all around looking for us." Phil continued, "We're in the alley between Good fellow and Union, right off of Page. How long till you can get here?" Gino was preparing to go before Phil could even say anything.

"I'll be there in 10 minutes; keep a lookout for me."

"Okay, we will, and bring a set of plates with you for the car."

"You're not planning on driving it, are you?"

"No, we'll park it, but you know, Dre's, not going to just leave his car; he's hoping that at least with different plates they might not find it as fast."

"I'm on my way," was the last thing Gino said, and they both hung up the phone.

Gino, as he was leaving made sure to have everyone on point. High-Top told him what happened on Garfield and he didn't want to take the chance of anything else happening. He went outside and started his trusty Chevy van, his favorite ride and his most dependable. This van had more money dumped into it than most tuner cars, it was not only fast it was powerful as hell; it was like having a tank with nitro in it. Within minutes, he was on his way.

Phil cautiously walked up the alley making sure that no police took notice of him, the last thing he wanted to do was lead the police back to his boys. Phil would have much rather taken a bullet himself, than be responsible for getting any member of his crew caught up. He was only gone about 15 minutes, yet it seemed as if he was gone for at least an hour.

He was approaching the garage when he saw Reggie peeping out the door. A look of relief came over Reggie's face as he realized that they were one step closer to getting out of this shit. Phil entered the garage and told Dre the good news.

"Gino will be here in a few. He said everything was cool as far as he knows; he hasn't heard anything about any other problems."

"That makes it sound like they were looking to get

to one of us," I said, wondering how true this statement might be.

Hot-Rod turned to me. "You mean to tell me this is over some bitch shit?" He knew we had very few enemies anymore.

We had been in control of the city for some time now, and each of us made sure to stay in good standings with our customers as well as our neighbors. As I thought about that very fact, I couldn't help but say aloud,

"Who the fuck is out to get us?"

It seemed to take forever, but Gino did finally arrive to pick us up. He backed into the garage next to my car and got out. He had one of his workers named Festus with him, and he got out on the passenger side of the van with a car cover and a lock set. Festus stayed at the garage to not only hide the car, but also keep an eye on it.

Our luck was so good that we just happened to pull into a garage that was just a few houses down from where he lived. I told him, "Pay the owner storage fees and keep an eye on my shit." Even though I did not know him very well, Gino trusted him, and that was good enough for me.

Festus started installing the lock as the rest of us piled into the van and went to Gino's house to figure out what the fuck was going on.

"Lott, Mike, and Tank should be at my house when we get there," Gino told me as he pulled out of the garage. "He's bringin' Alpo and Bake with him."

"How did he find out so fast?" I wanted to know.

"He said Mike heard it on the scanner."

"Fuck, did he say how bad it was?"

"He said it was bad, but they don't have any names, and they didn't get your plate number."

"That's good, but we still lost a couple guys; I hope they don't tie them to us," Phil said from the back seat.

"We need to get someone on damage control."

"Good idea," I said. "Good idea."

We all sat quietly as Gino drove to his house. You would have thought we were having a Welcome Home party when we drove up to Gino's house. There was a smile on almost every face there. We were at war, but because of how close we were to each other, I think it was more of a relieved look than anything else.

As we got out of the car, I noticed Lott and Mike's cars outside, it was a welcomed sight, and I was glad to see my top men there. I knew I was supposed to have a meeting the next morning but a meeting now was just as good. When we got in the house, I had Reggie call High-Top, so he could come to Gino's house. He got there about 30 minutes later.

"The first thing I want to say is that I'm sorry about our losses, and I want someone to make sure that our men's families are sent flowers and helped with any funeral expenses." That was my first order. "The second thing I'm really happy about is that everyone else is okay."

Everyone was happy, sad and angry at the same time. We had been hit at home, in an area where we should feel the safest; there was no way this was over.

A phone rang, and even though we had a rule about cell phones during times of trouble, High-Top thought it was important enough to answer.

"What's up, nigga? What's the word?" he said as he got up and left the room. Everyone continued to talk as High-Top was in the other room, and it seemed that we all had the same thing on our mind. Hot-Rod lit a Kool.

"Does anybody have the slightest clue as to who the fuck did this shit?"

Reggie rubbed his chin as if he was thinking about something. "I know I've seen that red Caddie somewhere before; I just can't think of where."

"And I know I've seen that dumb-ass Donald dude around my way before," said Phil.

I was starting to get even more upset, and even

though I didn't want to take it out on my men. I couldn't help but yell, "How the fuck can someone recognize a car or a person and not remember who they are? What the fuck kind of organization is this? We're drug dealers; we pay attention to anything and everybody! That's how we survive!" Deep inside, I knew I should not have yelled at them like that; we were all grown men and wanted to be treated like it.

"I'm sorry men, I don't mean to yell, but we need to be more careful and really pay attention to shit right now," They all looked at me because they knew what I was saying was true, "or we could all end up dead or caught up."

Things were tense in the room as we did our best to figure out what the fuck was going on. Hot-Rod stood up. "Does anyone want a drink?"

Several of us said yes and told him what we wanted. He went to the bar in the corner and started making drinks. As I looked over at him I couldn't help but laugh a li'. "Look at this drug-dealing bartender." The fucked-up thing was that he was damn good at it, too.

Hell I would rather have him make a drink for me than any other bartender I have ever come across. I walked over to the bar and waited for my drink, while I stood there I listened to several of the mens' conversations, hoping that I would hear at least one thing that would help me figure what the hell was going on.

Hot-Rod began to pour my drink. He looked at me. "Hen Dog and Pep, two cubes of ice coming up."

He was what I considered a true friend, and always knew just how to lighten the mood. I looked at him and laughed. "Thanks."

Hot-Rod passed me the drink, and right away I took a sip out of it. The rest of the crew who wanted drinks came over and picked them up off the bar. I looked at Hot-Rod. "Well, my nigga, what do we do now?"

"We do what we always do, buckle down and handle our shit."

He was right; we always managed to come out on top, but for some reason this seemed different. It had been so long since we had any real problems. "You're right; I guess I forgot."

Phil walked up to us. "Fuck you, nigga, you never forget shit."

I smiled at my friend. "That's only because I have the best crew in the world by my side." I always made sure that they knew I considered them my equals, and I never thought of myself as being better than any of them.

We continued to drink and talk for a while, yet nobody had a clue who was behind the attack on us. For some reason the mood in the room had really lightened, I think everyone felt a lot safer being together now. They say that there is safety in numbers, but I think there is safety with friends. I trusted these men with my life, and they trusted me with theirs, we were going to get to the bottom of this if it was the last thing we did. I couldn't let another one of my men go down. Ant was not one of my top men, but he was really doing his best to get there, and it really pisses me off when I think about the fact that he was now gone.

"You've got to be bullshittin' me! There's no way!" High-Top said into his phone as he returned into the room. I turned to him immediately. "What's wrong?"

He looked me right in my eyes. I know who it is, I know who's out to get us."

The room got so quiet you could have heard a dime bag drop. Everyone looked at him and waited for the rest.

I calmly asked him, "Who is it?"

He finally said, "It's Ericka and Manny."

Just about everyone in the room knew these two, and most of us had done shit for them, shit to help them get on their feet. This information could not be right. There was no way they would do this shit.

Hell, I thought they were down with us. I looked at Hot-Rod.

"Looks like we have to get to work," he responded.

"Against someone that we were trying to help." I stood in the middle of the room. "Today, at this moment, we are declaring war." I hated war, but it had to be done. "We're going to hit these mother fuckers so hard that they won't know what happened."

None of us wanted to fight someone so low on our radar, but if we didn't fight now we would look weak, and that, I wasn't going to let that happen.

I announced, "We found out what we needed to know. It's time to get out of here. But I want everyone to watch their backs; we don't want shit to happen tonight. We'll regroup in the morning at the yard."

We all finished our drinks and began to leave.

I returned home to my castle, my kingdom. I had done many things in my life, gone to the army, worked many jobs, lots of hustles, but with all that I did take the time to find me a good woman that would be there for me no matter what.

Her name was Gin just like the drink and she was

intoxicating, she was a li'l short woman with long hair and a body sexy enough to drive most men wild. At first glance, most would think she was a li'l scared woman trying to hang with the thugs, but those that knew her, knew she would put a bullet in a motherfucker just as fast as the L.A.P.D.

Gin was standing in the kitchen, making her favorite drink, hot chocolate. She was looking just as sexy as ever, and that was just what I needed after a day like today. She turned and looked at me as I came into the room, she gave me that li'l sexy smile that she had given me so many times before.

"Hello, baby, how was your day?"

No matter how bad my day had been I always said, "Not bad, but much better now."

I always told her what was going on, but never right away; I don't know if it was so that I didn't worry her, or if it was just because I enjoyed our daily ritual.

She knew something was wrong, but she never rushed me to tell her anything. She walked over to me and gave me that gentle li'l kiss that I looked forward to every day.

Gin had a way of getting me heated up, and as usual, she was doing it. She would kiss and rub on me in a way that would get any man hard and ready, and this time was not any different. She stepped back and took off her blouse; the only thing I could do was wrap my lips around one of those beautiful nipples and suck on it like a newborn baby.

I put my hand up her skirt and began to finger that hot, wet pussy. We never even made it up to the bedroom; instead, we made wild and passionate love on the living-room couch. With every thrust of her hips, she took me further away from reality, further into my world were everything was perfect.

After yet another hot sexual session, the two of us lay on the couch and held each other. I knew if I told her what happened today, and who was behind it she would be ready to go handle things right away, so I waited. I don't know why I did it, maybe it was just a moment of stupidity, but I picked up the remote and turned on the television. The first thing that came on was a news update, and right away Gin took notice.

"WHAT THE FUCK?" she yelled as she sat up, looking big eyed at the TV, "Is that..."

Before she could finish her question, I softly said, "Yes."

CHAPTER SIX

It had been a few weeks since anything major had happened, but there had been several smaller events going on. Gino, had a couple of his workers robbed; Hot-Rod, had a couple of his houses burned down. Nevertheless, other than that, nothing to worry about.

Alpo and Bake had made several runs for us without any problems, and we were stocked up on shit, so I figured it was time to give the two of them a li'l down time here in the city. Alpo just told me that he met some girl down on the river front and he wanted to take her out to dinner or something, maybe even take her to that steakhouse he saw over on Grand Avenue.

I had no problem with him going out, hell we all did it, I just wanted everybody to watch their backs. Can you believe that motherfucker Bake even found some freak to give him some, I know there was someone for everyone, but Bake, I never would have thought it.

For the most part, Hot-Rod, had been spending the last few weeks with his wife, Nefra, and their three kids. We all wanted to play tough, but we knew that at any moment we could be taken out, after all we were at war so, whenever possible, we tried to spend some time with our families.

He did his best to keep his family away from the shit, as a matter of fact we all did, nothing would be worse than something happening to our kids. Yea, we all had kids, hell I had five kids myself, and Gino had three.

Hot-Rod sat in the corner and watched his kids playing. Nefra walked into the room and almost instantly, she could see that her man had something on his mind.

"What's wrong?" she asked him as she sat on the chair beside him.

He sat silently for a moment before looking in her eyes. "Nothing."

"Don't lie to me, Rodney." She never called him by his street name.

"Well, the thing is," he looked at his kids, "I think I'm ready to get out of this shit."

Nefra never thought she would hear something like this come out of his mouth. "Are you sure that's what you want?" Praying that he would say yes, she just waited.

He thought for a minute before answering her. "Yes, I am, but I'm just not sure what I'll have to do to get out of it."

That scared her. "What do you mean by that?"

"When we started this shit, I was the one that said once you're in, it's forever; now I want out. How the hell is that going to look to the rest of the crew?"

"I don't care about them; I care about us," she said to him.

"I know, baby doll. "He often called her that. "Just remember, those guys are my family, too."

The crew meant a lot to Hot-Rod, but his wife and kids meant more, and I would not have wanted it any other way. We were all family; at least we tried to be, so I understood how he was feeling, even though he had yet to say anything to me about it. I needed Hot-Rod in this crew; he had a good head on his shoulders, and he was often the reason things went as smoothly as they did. I knew a while ago that he was ready to get out, but I was a selfish nigga. I wasn't ready to let him go.

I hadn't been back home in a couple of days and

I knew Gin was pissed, not because she thought I was out doing anything, but because the kids were driving her crazy. My kids would make the average person go crazy, with some of the shit, they did, and they had a way with Gin.

My youngest daughter, Andalia was the biggest job. She was what many called, "Hell on earth."

I called home to let Gin know how things were going. "Hey, baby girl, what's going on?"

"Nothing, but these kids are driving me crazy."

"Is everything still quiet?"

"Yes."

"I'll be home soon, baby."

"I know, I know. I love you, and I'll see you when you get home," she said, and hung up the phone. Gin knew how these trips out of town were; she just worried about me.

Even though things had been quiet, it was time that we made a li'l noise. I wasn't going to let Ericka get away with the shit she did. I just had to let the heat die down some before I made my move.

We had come up with several ideas about how to take care of our problems, but the best idea came from Phil. "Fuck beatin' around the bush; let's just go hit that bitch's head up."

He was right; the best way was the most direct

way. We had taken out several of her small time helpers, but it was bout time we got back to work, and finish what we set out to do...take Ericka out.

Phil, Reggie, and High-Top spent the last few weeks not only gathering men, but also gathering guns. We wanted every one in our crew to be ready for whatever. I don't know why but we all thought, the more guns the better, so we did everything we could to make sure we had the most guns.

As Lott and I headed back up to St. Louis, we both knew that shit was about to hit the fan. It was finally time to take care of Ericka, and once we started, there was no turning back. We rode for several miles just looking at nothing but the highway in front of us.

I hated the idea that everyone was just fighting to make me happy, so I had to ask, "Are you sure you're ready for this?"

"I'm ready for whatever."

We didn't know what kind of army Ericka had, so we really didn't know what to expect.

"Things could get pretty fuckin' bad before it's all over."

Lott looked at me. "I know, but we can't let her get away with shit. We'll take care of her. Just a couple more days, and shit'll be on and poppin'."

"Well, it's about fuckin' time; we should have been handling this shit."

"I know," was all I could say, because he was right.

I never liked to rush into shit, but this was one time I was bullshittin'. It's not because I was scared, but I was going up against what used to be a friend. I really wanted to make sure we did shit right; we could not afford to fuck up against someone that knew us.

Bake and Alpo decided to get together and take their new pussy out for dinner. They arrived at the "Best Steakhouse," around 7 p.m.; this place really lived up to its name. They had the best steaks in the Lou. They both wanted to impress their dates, so the told the women to order whatever they wanted.

"Oh, sh, sh, sh, shit, I forg, g, g, g, I forgot. Alpo this is my girl, Tay, and T, T, T, Tay, this is Alpo."

"Oh, yea, this is my friend, Maria. Maria, this is my nigga Bake, and you heard her name, so I don't need to tell you that."

The four of them sat in the back corner of the restaurant chillin', trying to get to know each other better. The conversations were simple and to the point. They all wanted to know where the other was from, and about past relationships.

Alpo did most of the talking for Bake, just so he didn't have to hear the stuttering.

"Well, we're from a small town in Pennsylvania called York. We have a few friends down here, so we come down and kick it with them from time to time."

"Really, who are they? Maybe we know them."

"Damn, girl, you sound like *Five-O* or something, askin' names and shit," Alpo said, laughing.

"It's not like that; we just wanted to know if we knew any of your friends," Maria said almost as if she was offended.

"I was just joking, girl; I didn't mean to hurt your feelings."

"I'm just tired of niggas always thinking, just because a bitch ask about something, that she up to no good," Tay said.

"Okay, okay, okay. Well, do you know a nigga named Dre, or Hot-Rod, or Gino, or how about a nigga named Lott?"

"Are we in St. Louis? Of course, we know them. I don't believe you really know them. Those niggas is big timers."

"W, w, w, well, don't fuckin' a, a, a, ask, then, if you don't want to know."

They all looked at Bake as if they were amazed

that he could speak. Before he could say anything else, Alpo said to the women, "So tell us about yourselves. Who do you know?"

CHAPTER SEVEN

It was an unusually cool night, when we decided to make our first strike against Ericka. High-Top had gotten us all the info we needed to know about her, we knew where she lived as well as where she played.

We didn't really want to get anybody innocent caught up in our shit so we decided to hit up her man Matt at his house first. I didn't know how she would react after we took out one of her main men, but I was hoping it would put a li'l fear in her.

We never realize just how bad things are until we see those around us dropping dead. I wanted to let Ericka to know that she fucked with the wrong niggas this time, I wanted her to think about the fact that every breath she took could be her last.

We had a hell of a crew going in on this, everyone lookin' forward to a li'l target practice. Mike, Tank,

Phil, Gino, along with a few people from his crew and me. I also called in a couple of heavy hitters, Bliss and his woman, Jane, that I met when I was in Philly a few years before, and these mother fuckers were crazy as hell.

I remember the first time I saw them in action, Jane stuck a broomstick up the ass of this crackhead named Becky because she looked at Bliss the wrong way. Bliss was crazy, but Jane was insane. From that day on, I learned to say, "ma'am," when talking to Jane, and I never let her get near a broom when I was around.

"Let's go, motha fuckas!" Tank yelled, his voice rumbling through the house. "It's time to work for that money you been makin'." Everybody treated it as if it was a game, but we knew there was nothing more serious than what we were about to do.

Phil walked up with a crazy smile on his face and looked at Mike. "I can't wait for this shit to jump off." He loved this shit more than he loved his woman.

Mike did not know what to say; he never enjoyed killing. He just did it so well, many of us figured he had to like it because he took such pride in it. While almost looking at the ground he said, "Me either, man; me either."

We had about five cars as we rolled on out, we never packed the cars with too many people at one time, just in case something happened. We were very cautious when it came to doing shit; sometimes it just paid to be that way. You know what they say, "Better safe than sorry." Never had there been a statement so true.

This was going to be an easy late night hit, it was about two a.m. on a Monday morning there's no way anyone would be expecting us. It would take us about 45 minutes to drive to Matt's place, he lived in a three-bedroom house with his girlfriend and her sister in south St. Louis, and we were in St. Charles at Tank's house.

"We should be there no later than three, right?" Tank asked Mike.

"I hope so," Mike said in response, knowing deep down inside he did not want to be involved in this shit.

"Do you think he'll be alone?" Mike looked at Tank, wondering why this man was really so concerned. They had been friends for most of their lives, and he had never known him to ask so many questions. Mike shook his head and smiled gently. He knew doubting his friend was crazy. Maybe this shit was really starting to get to him; it was time to get control of his emotions, and he didn't want to go around looking at his friends crazy.

As we drove down Highway 70, I turned and looked in the back seat only to see Jane wiping down two chrome .38s. Bliss didn't like pistols much, he was holding on to a pretty ass, gold plated, AK-47 with about 10 banana clips, he looked like he was going to do everything by himself. These two were ready for anything; the funny thing was that Jane was more eager to kill someone than Bliss, or anyone else in the whole crew.

She was the only female other than Gin that I trusted to handle her business.

"Are you ready?" I asked them.

"Of course we are," Bliss said, with a big-ass smile on his face.

"Even if he's not, I am, so let's get this shit going," Jane said, trying to make things speed up.

I laughed at her. "We'll be there soon enough. Just be patient. You'll be seeing blood before you know it." The mention of blood seemed to calm her down, so she sat back and stared out the window at the highway as we continued our journey.

Phil had decided to ride with Gino since he always had a better relationship with him than any of the others, the only one he was closer too was me.

"What's up with the party tomorrow?" Phil asked him, speaking of the birthday party Gino was having for his girlfriend, Teasha.

"Be there around 8, and you better bring a big-ass gift; I know you been makin' that money over on the north side, nigga."

They both laughed hard as hell, like they always did when they were together. They truly were brothers in the game, and they really enjoyed each other's company.

"The only way I can do that is if you tell me what to get her." Phil knew Teasha was fussy as hell. If he did not bring something she wanted, there was no sense in bringing anything.

Gino looked at him and smiled. "Just bring jewelry: gold, diamonds, or something. Nothing else seems to make her happy unless you're going to give her a stack of cash."

Laughter broke out again, and Phil said, "That might just be a good idea."

"No, don't do that; I wanted to give her cash. It's better than taking her out shopping."

Phil laughed so hard tears began to come out his eyes.

"You mother fuckers better be ready for this shit," D-Dog said to his brothers that he had riding with him. D-Dog, Paul, John, and Danny were brothers that did everything together; they had been working for Gino around eight months. You could never find one of them without finding at least one of the others with him.

They did what they could just to be a part of the crew, but we never let them do too much until tonight. This would be their test; if they can pass this, they would have a guaranteed job.

"So, do you think this is it, bro? Is it finally going down tonight?" Paul asked his older brother D-Dog.

"After tonight we'll be in fa sho."

John said harshly, from the back of the van, "Fuck ya'll. I been in. I just didn't want to hurt ya'll feelings."

Danny laughed. "And I got him in." All the brothers enjoyed a good laugh, while deep inside they all knew this might be their last.

Austin and Brandon were in the last car with a couple girls that Gino had in his squad named Dena and Brooklyn. All four of these young bucks were crazy. These young fuckers were the ones Gino would use when he needed to send a message to someone, he sent them to collect some money from this motherfucker named Black Jake, and they did a lot more than just collect.

Gino and I were out with our women at a sports bar when a news flash came on, and what we saw was just crazy. These fools did not kill the nigga.

They cut his fucking hands off and left him downtown on the steps under the Arch.

Later that night we asked them what the fuck they were thinking.

"If he can't put his hands in his pocket and pay you, he damn sure won't be able to put his hand in his pockets to pay himself."

Gino and I could do nothing but look at each other and smile. They had a good point. From that day on whenever we needed to send a message to someone, we sent them.

"Do you think that Dre will make us full members after this?" Brooklyn whispered to Dena in the back seat.

Dena looked at her. "We are full members. What the fuck are you talking about?"

"I want to get our own crew, so we can tell somebody to do shit for us."

Dena laughed. "We can do that now, but who wants all the hassle of keeping up with shit like that? I don't."

Brandon looked back at the girls. "Ya'll bitches need to shut the fuck up with that crazy shit."

Austin angrily barked, "I don't know about the rest of ya'll, but I'm fuckin' happy, so if you don't like what's going on I think you need to get the fuck out."

No one wanted to be around Austin when he was angry, and they really didn't want to be the reason he was pissed, so they all decided to sit quietly for the rest of the ride.

Our little caravan moved down the highway at a steady pace, we were on our way to take care of business and after tonight, things were probably going to get a li'l hot around town. All I could do was hope that everything would go smoothly and none of my people would get hurt, that included me.

After about 45 minutes we were pulling off the highway about six blocks from our final target. I said in almost a whisper to the rest of the people in the car with me, "I hope everyone's ready,"

Bliss laughed. "You know damn well you got the best fuckin' crew around. Everybody's ready, man. Stop trippin'."

I knew he was right, but for some reason, I couldn't help but worry. Something just didn't feel right. I just couldn't figure out what it was.

We pulled up in front of a li'l brick house that sat slightly back off the street. It almost looked as if the house was empty until I noticed the light from a television in the front room. I could see at least two shadows moving around, so I knew at least that many people were about to die.

I had the young bucks, D-Dog and his brothers go around back, they knew exactly when to bust in. Phil and Gino took the left side, while Mike and Tank went to the right side of the house, just in case anyone tried to get out that way. I had Bliss, Jane, Austin, Brandon, Dena, and Brooklyn with me and we were going straight in the front door blasting.

We snuck up to the front of the house, making sure not to ruin our surprise attack. We paused for a second, just to make sure that everybody was in place and ready.

I looked back at Bliss and he had the biggest shit-eatin' grin on his face, then for some reason he was not smiling any more. I turned to look in front of me, and before I could turn completely around, I heard what sounded like the loudest clap of thunder that I have ever heard before.

Then all I could hear was Austin's voice yelling out, "OH SHIT!"

What the fuck? They knew we were coming.

CHAPTER EIGHT

Hot-Rod and High-Top sat just down the street from Ericka's loft, where they were hoping to get some more info about her, in order to make their job easier when it was time to take her out.

They both paid close attention when she came out, went in the trunk of her green Geo Storm, and went back in.

"There she is," Hot-Rod said to High-Top.

"I see her."

"Could you see what she got out of her trunk?"

"All I could see is that it was big and black." High-Top paused for a second before finishing. "Maybe that bitch decided to get a dick that would fit in her sloppy-ass pussy." Both of them laughed so hard that they wondered if anyone heard them.

Just as Ericka set her package down in the

corner of the living room her phone rang. She paused as if she wasn't sure she wanted to answer, and then walked over to the phone. "Hello."

A voice on the other end of the phone said, "We need to talk."

Ericka could not figure out who the voice belonged to. "Who the fuck is this?" she asked.

For a few seconds the voice said nothing, then from out of nowhere, "Just call me a friend."

"I don't have any friends."

"You do now."

Ericka thought for a minute. "What do we need to talk about, anyway?"

It was almost as if the person was getting pissed off. "Bitch, do you want to keep breathing?"

Even though Ericka knew it wasn't a threat, what she just heard scared the shit out of her. "What do you mean?"

"I'm fuckin' trying to keep you alive, dumb ass."

"Okay, what do you want?"

"Meet me on the London and Sons parking lot, the one on Grand Avenue, in 90 minutes."

"How will I know you?" she asked the voice.

The last thing Ericka heard the voice say before hanging up was, "Don't worry about that; I'll know you. Come alone." Then the phone went silent.

Hot-Rod sat quietly and rubbed his head as if he had a headache, suddenly he felt a slap on his shoulder from High-Top. "There she is," he said.

Hot-Rod looked up and took notice of Ericka getting into her car. "I think the bitch is leaving."

"Should we follow her?"

"Of course."

Ericka backed out of her driveway and headed towards the highway, with Hot-Rod and High-Top following closely behind her.

"Where the fuck, do you think this bitch is going?" High-Top asked Hot-Rod.

"I don't know but she's headed towards downtown," Hot-Rod said. "We'll just have to keep following her and see."

"Should we call Dre?"

Hot-Rod looked at High-Top. "Are you fuckin' crazy? Did you forget what Dre is doing?"

"Oh, shit. That's right."

"It's a good thing I'm with you; you'll fuck around and get somebody killed."

High-Top knew he'd said something stupid so he just sat quietly and said nothing.

Ericka was driving almost 100 miles per hour, she was scared, and so she never noticed the dark blue Lexus following closely behind her. The only thing she could think of was the fact that she was in some sort of danger, and she had no idea how, even though she did have an idea why.

The only person that she could think of was Dre, but why would he wait so long? It had been months since she had heard anything from any of her people on the streets. Then it hit her like a brick, why hadn't she heard anything from any of her people, what was going on, and who was this person that she was going to meet? She could do nothing but think about what was going to happen when she met her so-called, friend, and more importantly, who the fuck was this person?

Hot-Rod pulled a little closer to Ericka, but he made sure that she still did not see him behind her. He watched as she moved over to the exit lane for Grand Avenue, then he did the same, both exited the highway with only a couple of cars between them. As they began to head north on Grand, High-Top noticed a car that looked familiar to him.

"Isn't that..." And he stopped as if he was scared to finish.

"Isn't that what, motha fucka?" Hot-Rod said to him.

"I thought I saw a car I recognized."

Hot-Rod looked at him. "Well, who the fuck was it?"

"I don't know for sure; I just know the car from somewhere."

Even though Hot-Rod did not want to admit it, he knew that if High-Top thought he recognized something or someone, chances are he really did.

Ericka pulled into the London and Sons parking lot, and Hot-Rod and High-Top pulled into the Exxon parking lot across the street; they made sure to park in a spot where they could not be seen, but they could see everything. They sat for what seemed to be at least an hour and watched as Ericka just sat in her car.

"She must be waiting for someone," Hot-Rod said, almost in a whisper.

High-Top said impatiently, "Why don't we go kill that bitch?"

"We can't."

"Why the fuck not?"

"Because, Dre wouldn't want us to do it like that." Hot-Rod knew that all things came in time, and even though part of him wanted to kill her now, this wasn't the time, and it damn sure wasn't the place.

Ericka sat with the music blasting; she was so deep in thought that she did not notice the hooded young man that was walking up to her car. As she lit her Kool, the young man tapped on her window and scared her so bad that she dropped her cigarette in her lap. She looked at him as he motioned for her to let her window down.

She slowly eased her hand down beside her until she could feel the cold blue steel of her .38 in her grasp. She let her window down only enough to speak to the person. "Who the fuck are you?"

"I'm your friend," he said with a smile.

"I don't have any friends."

"Well, you can call me your life saver."

She didn't want him to think he was in control of the conversation, but at the same time, she really wanted to hear what he had to say. Ericka tried to force a smile. "So what do you want to talk to me about?"

The young man looked around for a second. "I can help you take Dre and his crew out."

Ericka's heart felt as if it had skipped a beat or two, and she did her best not to show too much excitement. She thought for a moment. "And what do you want for this?"

"Can I get in and talk to you?" he said.

She reluctantly said, "Yes, get in."

"Do you see that?" Hot-Rod said to High-Top.

"Of course I do, but I can't tell who the fuck it is with that fuckin' hood on."

"I hope we didn't just follow this bitch all the way over here just so she could find a dick to suck on," Hot-Rod said angrily.

"Do you really think that's what she's doing?"

"I really don't know, but what I do know is that this bitch is a freak, so there's no telling what the fuck she's trying to do."

High-Top didn't think that was the case, but he sat silently and watched as the hooded man walked around and got into the passenger side of Ericka's car.

The young man looked at Ericka. "I'll help you take Dre out, and all I want in return is one neighborhood to call my own."

Ericka knew that if she made this deal it would be like making a deal with the devil. She already didn't trust this person, so even if she gave him her word, she would have to kill him to make sure he never turned against her. She looked him square in his eyes. "If that's all you want, you've got a fuckin' deal."

A smile came across the young man's face as he thought about the fact that he was about to be his own boss. He would have control of his own neighborhood, and later he would take Ericka out as well.

"Is there anything else?" she asked him.

"No, but watch your ass because they're watching you."

Startled, she said, "How do you know this? As a matter of fact, how can you get close enough to Dre to take him out?"

The young man was no longer smiling when he looked at her. "Because I work with him; he considers me a friend."

Ericka was immediately disgusted with this guy, just the thought of someone turning on a friend like that, she knew she had to kill him as soon as her business with him was done.

She wanted Dre dead but she had a real reason, this asshole was just being greedy because she knew that Dre took good care of his people.

She thought very hard as the young man got out of her car, part of her wanted to kill him now, but she had to, at least wait until she had no further use for him. Ericka pulled out of the parking lot, paying closer attention to her surroundings. As she turned and headed back to the highway she noticed a dark-blue Lexus parked slightly behind the gas station with two people in it, and remembered the warning that her new "friend" had just given her.

She wasn't sure, but she thought she saw that

car in her neighborhood earlier that same day. She wondered to herself, "Could these guys be the ones watching me?" She headed home, keeping her eyes in her rearview mirror hoping not to see a blue anything following her.

Hot-Rod followed a li'l further back than normal, but deep inside he knew it was no use; he somehow knew that Ericka had seen them. He followed her all the way home. Ericka pulled into her driveway. She continued to sit in her car for a few minutes. Then she got out and looked directly at the blue Lexus and waved as if to say, "Fuck you! I know you're following me."

The thought of this bitch taunting them had pushed Hot-Rod over the edge; he grabbed his gun, cocked it, got out of the car.

"Let's finish this shit right now." High-Top could see the anger in his eyes as they marched down the street to shut this bitch up for the last time.

CHAPTER NINE

A phone rings on a cluttered desk, the lights are dim because it was late and at first it appeared that, no one was around. As the ringing continues, a door in the back corner of the room opens and a tall, slim, well-dressed, young, white guy enters.

This man looked to be in his mid-to-late twenties with a five o'clock shadow that looked to be a couple days old. He went to the phone and snatched it up.

"Narcotics squad, Detective Dustin Sellers, how may I help you?"

"Do you still give rewards for info about drug dealers?" the voice asked on the other end of the phone.

Puzzled, Sellers said, "Yes, we do."

After a few seconds the person continued, "I need to talk to someone about this guy selling drugs near my house."

"That's what I'm here for," said Sellers. "What do you want to tell me?"

"Well, there's this guy and his friends selling drugs around the corner from my house, and I want something done about it now."

"Is there any way you can come in and file a complaint?"

The caller angrily said, "NO!"

Sellers thought for a second. "How can I help you if you don't file a complaint?"

The phone went silent for a moment. "What if I tell you their names and where they are? Will that help?"

Sellers agreed to see what he could do, and took down all the information that the caller gave him. The police had been trying to find out everything they could about a group of mostly guys, that appeared to have control of the drug distribution in the city, for a long time now. They had often heard names and locations mentioned, but could never find any real leads, or anything that tied any one person to anything.

Sellers had somehow found the one person in the entire city that was willing to talk and help the police tie up some loose ends. The C.I. had given Sellers so many names and locations, that he wondered if somehow, they themselves were a li'l closer to this group than they wanted him to know.

Sellers sat at his desk and looked over the notes he had taken while on the phone. The only thing he could think was, "This time we'll get these fuckers, and I just hope this woman will testify."

After carefully looking over everything, he finally called his partner, Byron "B-More" Goode. Goode was a lot shorter than his partner was, but his attitude was bigger than a bear's. Some would say he had the li'l man's complex; he often would find the biggest perps in the streets and take them down as hard as he could, just to show everyone that he could.

"Yo, Goode, I just got a lead," Sellers said into his radio.

After a couple of minutes, Goode responded with an eager, "Let's go then; I'll be up in a sec."

Sellers knew Goode would be happy to hear the news, but he really didn't expect what happened next. Before he could even stand up from his desk and put his jacket on, Goode came running through the door as if he was being chased. "Okay, man, let's go."

Sellers looked at him and laughed. "Slow down, officer. Can I at least put my jacket on first?"

Goode wiped the sweat from his forehead. "Hell no, fuck that jacket. Does it look like I'm cold?" Sellers just shook his head, grabbed his jacket, and the two detectives headed out to see just how much the new C.I. really knew.

As they left the building, Sellers had finally found something else to think about. He was liked by almost every other police officer that knew him, but for some reason Goode had a hard time even getting someone to say so much as hello to him. Between the two of them, Goode had been a detective the longest, almost ten years.

Sellers had just made detective a few months ago, but he was always treated as if he was the old-timer. As two uniformed officers, named Milo and Rob walked past, they made sure to speak to Sellers, but neither of them even acknowledged Goode in any way. Sellers said his hellos, and he and his partner continued to their car.

"What the fuck, man?" Sellers said to Goode, who had just pulled out a cigarette and lit it.

Goode exhaled smoke. "What? Am I supposed to know what you're talking about?"

"Why does it seem like everybody hates you?"

"Man, fuck them. They're all just fuckin' jealous."

"Of what?"

"It's not important; it happened years ago, and I'm through talkin' about it."

Sellers was not happy with the response he just got from his partner, something just did not feel right. He decided to let the conversation end for now, they had bigger fish to fry, and besides, he could see that Goode was upset now.

Two super cops, that's what they liked people to think about them, at least Sellers did. Goode had decided to drive for a change and Sellers wasn't mad at all, he did most of the driving, and was happy to be getting a break.

Goode pulled out of the central booking parking lot, and headed north, even though it was late night, they wanted to get a look at the area in question. They had almost made it to their destination, when they heard over the radio, a call about a shootout on the south side of the city. Even though it would take them several minutes to get there, they decided to go and see what was going on.

"It's been a few months since we had one of those," Sellers said to Goode.

Goode smiled. "I know, and we missed that one too."

Sellers laughed at his partner. "You never know; we might just get there, and it's still going on Robo-

Cop." Then he put the blueberry on top of the car, and the two of them were off to the races.

As they sped through traffic, Sellers got a little excited, himself. He had never been involved in a real shootout, and he was hoping, deep inside, that they would make it there in enough time to get a couple of shots off.

Goode had decided to take King's Highway because it would have less traffic this time of night. After about ten minutes of driving, the detectives were surprised to still hear heavy gunfire.

"This must be a hell of a shootout." Sellers said.

Even Goode was a bit stunned. "I know. I'm going to pull over so we can get our vest out."

As soon as they car slowed almost to a complete stop, they both had their doors open and were getting out of the car. As they started putting their Kevlar on, they both took notice of the fact that the shooting had seemed to intensify. Just as Sellers was about to say something about it, he noticed several cars speeding through an intersection a little more than a block away.

Realizing that his partner had also seen the cars, he asked, "Do you think we can catch them?"

Surprisingly Goode looked at Sellers and said something his partner had never heard him say before, "No, and there's no sense in trying either."

Sellers was a bit bewildered, but he decided that it would be more important to get to the scene to help their fellow officers anyway. The two of them jumped back in the car and sped off.

You could feel the tension in the car as Sellers and Goode sped towards the shootout, but the two of them also knew they were still several minutes away from the war zone. They were both excited but at the same time Sellers was feeling something that he didn't understand, he was actually scared and he didn't know why.

CHAPTER TEN

Bliss yelled out to Gino as he came from the side of the house, "They knew we were coming, look out!"

D-Dog and his brothers had gone in through the back door, and we could hear them shooting and yelling inside.

Mike and Tank were shooting it out with someone on the right side of the house while Phil continued to shoot at someone on the left side. It didn't look like we were going to be able to get in the front of the house at first but all of a sudden Brandon and Brooklyn seemed to be getting the best of the mother fuckers that came out at us.

Just as we were making our entry through the front door, we heard tires screeching down the street towards us.

"Austin, Dena, take them mother fuckers down!" I yelled out.

Just as they turned, Mike came out front. "I think they called for help."

"How do you know that?" said Bliss.

"A carload just pulled up out back, and that looks like a couple of their people coming down the street."

The brothers were inside the house, blastin' away at anything and everything that moved.

"If you come out now, we'll let you live," Paul yelled into the house, trying to draw everyone out into the open.

"Fuck you!" One of the people screamed back at him as they fired back towards him.

D-Dog dropped down and tried to sneak around the side of the room. Just then, he noticed the one person that they came to take out. He saw Matt over in the corner hiding under a table. He motioned for John to come over were he was. "There that fucker is."

John smiled at him. "I want to kill his ass, but Dre needs to see him first."

"I know, but he didn't say we couldn't shoot his ass in the leg or something," D-Dog said.

Just then I made it in with Bliss, Jane, and Dena.

"Go left!" I yelled to Bliss and Jane.

"Dena, go right with me!" We shot ourselves deeper into the house.

Dena fired a few shots, then looked at me. "This is a li'l harder than we thought it would be."

She was right, but I didn't want to admit it.

I could hear the shooting outside and it worried me, but I had to concentrate on what was going on right in front of me, I had to get to Matt. I could see D-Dog and his brothers in the middle room, there were about five or six more mother fuckers to take down, but I still hadn't seen Matt.

Brooklyn fired two shots into one of the people outside, and yelled, "I got another one!"

Brandon smiled at her. "So what? I got four of them already."

"Shut the fuck up and just keep shootin'!" Austin screamed at the two of them. He was young, but looked at this as a job, and didn't like the idea of them acting like it was a game.

"Fuck you," Brandon said. "It's just those last three mother fuckers over there."

"Make that two," Brooklyn said as she watched another one drop to the ground as his head seemed to explode from the bullet that just hit him.

"Go left," Tank said to Mike and Phil. Mike really didn't want to leave his friend's side while something like this was going on, but he knew Tank was right. It was the only way they would be able surround the people that pulled up out back.

"Tank, look out!" Phil yelled.

Sadly, Tank never heard him, as one of the guys came up behind him and put two shells into the back of his head.

Mike screamed, "Tank, no!" as he watched his lifelong friend's body go limp and fall to the ground. He jumped up, firing, and ran towards his friend's body.

"Mike, get down!" Phil begged. However, it was too late. Even though Mike had taken out his best friend's killer, he himself fell victim to his rage and took one bullet in his neck that seemed to turn him into a rag doll.

We had taken out everyone inside the house, or so I thought, but I still had not seen Matt.

"He's over here," John yelled to me.

D-Dog flipped over a table in the corner of the middle room to reveal Matt, scared and crying like a little bitch.

I walked over to Matt and smiled at him. "What's wrong, li'l boy? Do you want your mommy?"

Matt looked up and begged, "Please don't kill me, and I'll do whatever you want."

"Tell me what Ericka is up to. Why the hell is she fucking with us?"

"She never told us. All I know is that she's mad at you for some reason."

Bliss laughed and said, "Is this the gangsta bitch we came to kill? He's acting more like a gangsta snitch."

John kicked Matt in his face. "You don't look so tough to me."

"Let's kill this bitch," Danny said.

"Can I do it? Please," Jane pleaded.

I looked down at Matt's bloody face. "Do you like gangsta movies?"

With blood pouring out of his mouth, Matt looked up at me, confused. "Yes." He paused for a second. "Please don't kill me."

I turned to walk away. "One of my favorite movies is *The Godfather*, and in the words of Michael Corleone, 'I'm not going to kill you. Paul, kill him.'" The sound was so loud that it seemed as if the plaster was going to fall off the walls.

Brandon came around back just in time to take down the last asshole in the back. Brooklyn screamed as she came around back and saw Mike and Tank's bloody bodies lying crumpled on the ground. The rest of us that were inside the house came out of the back door.

The sight of two of my best men, lying on the ground dead was very unnerving. As bothered as we all were, we could hear the sirens getting close to us, so we got in our cars so we could get the hell out of there.

Just as we were pulling off, I could see three more cars coming down the street very fast. Part of me knew that it was more of Ericka's people coming to help Matt; little did they know they were far too late to do anything to help him now. Just as we got about two blocks away, Jane noticed several police cars headed towards Matt's house on one of the parallel streets.

Bliss made a statement. "Looks like somebody's going to get in trouble."

We all knew he was speaking of the rest of Ericka's men that showed up at Matt's house when we were leaving.

"Well, better them than us," Jane said with a smile.

I sat quietly as we headed back to Tank's house. After so many years of hustling together, I never thought that I would ever be preparing to have this conversation with his girlfriend and his sister. Even worse, I was going to have the same conversation with Mike's mom.

Both of them had kids, and I just didn't want to have to look those children in their faces, knowing that their dads died fighting with me, doing something for me. This was going to be one of the hardest things I ever had to do in my life, telling my friends families that their loved one were dead.

As we drove, I couldn't help but notice the way the sunrise was turning the sky red. "Just think, Mike and Tank will never see the sunrise again," I whispered.

Bliss patted me on my shoulder. "Neither will that mother fucker, Matt."

That thought alone at least made me feel a little better, but I knew that feeling wouldn't last much longer as we continued our journey. I sat looking out the window quietly; occasionally looking in the rearview long enough to make sure that the rest of my crew was still following closely behind me. One thing I always loved was riding on the highway, but this was one trip I really did not want to take.

CHAPTER ELEVEN

"How much more do we have drop to off?" Reggie asked Lott.

"About nine ounces," Lott said in response.

The two of them had been out most of the night delivering packages to our many workers around the city. The weed had already been distributed' all they had was a li'l "white girl" left to drop off.

"I hope everything went well with them guys last night," Lott said roughly.

Reggie looked at him. "They can handle themselves." He thought for a moment. "Besides, they have those two crazy mother fuckers from Philly with them."

Lott knew Reggie was right, yet he could not help but wonder about them. For some reason, he had a gut feeling that something was wrong. Lott drove out to Jennings to drop a few ounces to one of his workers, a twenty-year-old girl named Ayanna. She was a tall fine, tattooed chick. She was also a hothead that didn't mind shooting first, and asking questions later.

As they pulled up in front of her house, they saw her friend Holly standing in the front door. Reggie had a crush on Holly, but he did his best not to let anyone know. He rolled down his window and yelled out to her, "What the hell you doing out here, girl?"

Holly smiled at him. "Waiting on you."

Just the thought of her waiting on him made Reggie feel like a school boy.

"Well, Daddy's here now," he told her as he got out of the car.

Holly was a little skinny white girl with long, dirty-blond hair. She often tried to forget that she was not black, but Ayanna made sure to remind her every chance she got. Actually, if you did not know them, you would not have known they were friends. Ayanna walked up behind Holly as she was standing in the doorway, giggling.

"What's so funny?"

Holly didn't really like talking to her about Reggie, so she just responded with, "Nothing." Even though she didn't say anything about it, Ayanna had always known how Holly felt about Reggie. She just enjoyed making her squirm.

As Lott and Reggie got out of the car, they both walked to the trunk of the car. Lott opened the trunk and Reggie removed a small black book bag from it. It contained about five ounces of the best cocaine in St. Louis at the time. As they turned to go into the house Reggie couldn't help but feel that someone was watching him.

The two men walked into the house only to see Ayanna's boyfriend Sean, sitting on the couch rolling a blunt.

"What the fuck is this punk doing here?" Lott barked, looking Sean straight in his eyes.

Reggie looked at Ayanna angrily and said, "I thought we told you not to have this fool around when we were doing business."

Ayanna quickly said, "I told him he had to leave, but he wouldn't go." She was a tough bitch, but she always seemed to find guys that liked to beat up women. This li'l frail fucker weighed about 140 pounds if that. Yet somehow he seemed to be able to control this girl like he was as big as a house.

Reggie looked at Sean.

"Get your motha fuckin'-ass up, nigga, now." As much as Sean may have wanted to protest, he knew the safest thing for him to do was comply. He quickly hopped to his feet and left the house.

Reggie, still angry, smiled at Holly. "What's up, sexy?"

He had never spoken to her like this in front of Ayanna, so she really didn't know how to react. She shyly looked at him. "I'm doing fine now."

Lott was so pissed about the fact that Sean was there, he was considering not giving Ayanna anything. The only reason he didn't follow his first thought was that he knew that this girl and her friends made a lot of money. No matter how much shit he gave her, she would have all the money in a matter of days.

Reggie continued talking to Holly as Lott went into the kitchen with Ayanna to take care of business.

"So, when are you going to stop bullshitting and let me take you out or something?" Reggie said to Holly flirtatiously.

Holly felt like a queen; she never thought that this day would come. She looked up at him. "If you want, we can go out later on tonight."

Reggie was excited as he could be. He knew Holly liked him, but he never thought she would agree to go out with him. The two of them sat in the living room making plans for their first big date. They both really liked each other, but neither of them believed that this day would ever come.

Lott liked Ayanna, but not in a romantic way. He often thought of her as a daughter. The only thing that bothered him, was the fact that she always seemed to find losers as boyfriends.

He looked at her as she sat at the kitchen table weighing the cocaine. Lott really wanted to say something about Sean, but he didn't want to waste his time. As long as he had known her, she never listened to anyone's advice when it came to her personal life. And this time wouldn't be any different.

Reggie was happy to be receiving Holly's attention, but he just couldn't get the idea that someone was watching him out of his head. He walked over to the window and looked up and down the street. Even though he didn't see anything, he did feel something. It was something that he just could not shake. He continued his conversation with Holly, hoping that his gut was wrong.

Lott looked at Ayanna and he couldn't hold in what he was feeling any longer. "Why do you keep fuckin' with that fool?" he asked her.

A puzzled look came over Ayanna's face for a

moment. "I guess because I like light-skinned niggas."

This was one of the dumbest things Lott ever heard her say. He wanted to keep going, but he knew that it wouldn't matter. Even if he had continued to talk until he was blue in the face, she would still do what she wanted to do.

The house had become unusually quiet, as Reggie and Holly had gone outside, while Lott and Ayanna had nothing else to say to each other.

Reggie and Holly continued their flirtatious conversation as they sat on the front porch. Reggie still had a feeling of being watched, and Holly could see that something was wrong with him. She really cared about him and she hoped that he felt the same way about her. "What's wrong, baby?" she asked him.

Reggie was surprised that she noticed he had something on his mind. He looked at this fine young white girl, and couldn't help but feeling sorry for her. Deep inside Reggie knew that Holly shouldn't be involved in the drug game. She came from a li'l small town somewhere on the west coast, but somehow ended up in St. Louis. Everyone had asked her at one time or another why she left home, but for some reason she would never say. Reggie had a few ideas why she left home, and none of them were good. When he looked at her, all he saw was innocence, and purity. Somehow he knew deep inside, that he loved this girl, and he didn't want anything to happen to her.

Lott came out the door and mumbled. "Let's get the fuck out of here."

Reggie looked at Holly and smiled. "I'll see you later, baby." Then he turned and went to the car. As he got into the car he thought about telling Lott how he felt, but decided not to after seeing the anger in his face.

CHAPTER TWELVE

The shooting was all but over when Sellers and Goode arrived. It looked as if a small war had gone on, at this li'l south St. Louis home. There were at least twenty dead bodies both inside and outside of the house. Sellers had never seen a crime scene such as this. Goode was unaffected by what he was seeing, after all he had seen it many times before. From the looks of things they both might be seeing more mini war scenes as the days went on.

As the detectives walked through the crime scene, Goode began to realize that he had known several of the people that were now laying dead yet he didn't say anything. He continued to walk quietly without letting the anger inside of him show. Sellers was amazed, by what he was seeing. He had only heard about shit like this and never thought he would see it. Even though he had already knew the answer, the newness of it all caused him to look to Goode.

"What do you think happened here?"

Goode could barely hold in his anger, but he did manage to look at his young green partner. "It looks to me like a few people got shot."

Sellers, not knowing what to say after such a remark from Goode, who decided not to say anything else. That may have been the smartest thing he could do at the time.

Sellers could see that something was bothering Goode, and it wasn't just the norm. He had the feeling that his partner somehow knew more than he was admitting to. It was almost as if Goode had known these people. Sellers had finally began to notice some of the shit that he heard others whispering about when they saw his partner.

"What's on your mind, partner?" Sellers had to ask Goode. He wanted to ask so much more, but inside he had known that he wouldn't get a straight answer. Goode looked at this young white cop who was now staring him straight in his face.

"So many young people are dying in our streets, and we can't do a damn thing about it." Goode had never really shown any emotion when it came to his work. This time everyone could see that he was madder than usual. As he walked around the crime scene and looked at the bodies, he could be seen several times biting on his lip. He was one pissed-off cop, and no one wanted to get in his way.

Sellers had walked away from Goode and went back to the squad car. While he was there a call came over the radio that seemed to chill him to the bone. After several minutes, he got himself together and rushed to tell Goode what he heard.

Just as Sellers was about to enter the house, Goode rushed out. "Come on, let's go."

"But I heard on the radio..." Sellers tried to tell his partner.

"I know, I heard it too. We're going over there."

Sellers looked at him, "But that's not our jurisdiction."

Angrily Goode barked, "I don't give a fuck! Let's fuckin' go!"

The two men were in the car and on the way before anyone could say anything to them. Goode was driving as if he had a fire in him. Sellers wanted to say something, but decided the best thing to do was to remain silent. Little did he know, he was about to find out just what was bothering his partner. Sellers was a good cop, but he was about to be thrust into a situation that would test all that he was.

As the two detectives continued on their way Sellers noticed a tear in his partner's eye. He wanted to comment but again he decided not to say anything. Even as a young cop he knew that sometimes, the best thing you could do was just sit back and observe.

As Sellers and Goode pulled up in front of the eastside loft, Goode finally let it slip out. "If they touched him, I'll kill them myself!" he exclaimed.

In surprise Sellers said, "Who are you talking about?"

Goode thought for a long while before answering him. "My brother."

All Sellers could do was stare at his partner in disbelief. After all this time, was it true that his partner's brother was involved. He knew he was supposed to do something, but what? He dropped his head as if he was ashamed. "Is your brother involved in this shit, B-Mo?"

Even though he knew it could cause problems for him later, Goode decided to see if his young partner could handle the truth. He looked at the young detective and answered, "Yes, he is."

Not knowing just how his partner would handle

what he had just told him, Goode decided that this would be the last case Sellers would ever work on with him.

Goode really liked Sellers, but there was no way he could let him find out that he was involved with this group of thugs. Not only was he providing guns and drugs to his brother's crew, but he also did several shakedowns for them.

Goode had known me and my crew well. He had often shook us down when he needed a few extra dollars. It had become such a routine that I had decided to put him on his payroll.

Over the last few years Goode had made a lot of money with me, but for some reason he had gotten greedy. If only everyone had known that he was the one that recruited Donald "Dink" Dums to make the hit on me. Goode hooked up with Dums after arresting him for beating on his wife.

Dums was a stocky li'l nigga with a li'l bitty white girl for a wife. Goode had smacked his woman a time or two, but even he couldn't understand why Dums would beat on such a little woman as if she was a man. Goode really didn't like Dums, he considered him a bitch. As a cop Goode realized that if Dums did get killed, it was for the best.

Goode was more involved in this shit than he

wanted to be. He had to stop Sellers from figuring it out, he just had to figure out how. Sometimes the hardest thing to do was get rid of another cop.

Sellers began to feel a bit uncomfortable for some reason. He had the feeling that his partner was somehow connected to one of the bloodiest drug wars the city had seen in years. He knew that he would need to watch his back now. He had no idea how true this was. Goode wanted him out of the way, and he would soon find out just how bad.

CHAPTER THIRTEEN

It had been a couple weeks since that deadly night when I lost several of my closest friends. Little did I know while I was wondering how to break the news to Tank and Mike's families, there was another shootout going on just across the river.

Hot-Rod and High-Top had their own shit going on with Ericka. They had decided to deal with her themselves, but they didn't expect what would happen next.

As they approached Ericka they noticed a red dodge van approaching very fast. They had no idea that this was the beginning of one hell of a fight. The van pulled up behind Ericka's car and the doors swung open before the van came to a complete stop.

Right away Hot-Rod and High-Top took cover behind the cars that were parked near them. Hot-

Rod noticed Manny as he got out of the drivers side of the van. He never liked Manny, but he knew deep inside that it wasn't going to be easy to take him out.

High-Top yelled out to Hot-Rod as shots began to ring out in the quiet neighborhood, "It looks like about seven of them. You take the left side, I'll take the right. I think I saw Lee with them."

"Fuck that; get back to the car. I got something for them!" Hot-Rod screamed back. The two men moved back towards their car with military precision while ducking and dodging bullets the whole way.

As Hot-Rod made it to the car, he cautiously moved back to the trunk and opened it. Inside was a small blue bag that he pulled out carefully. A big smile came across Hot-Rod's face as he unzipped the bag. High-Top had no clue what was in the bag, but he knew it had to be something big just by the look on Hot-Rod's face.

High-Top almost fainted at the sight of the grenades that Hot-Rod pulled out of the bag. He always knew this nigga was crazy, he just never thought he was this crazy. Hot-Rod pulled the pin, stood up, and threw the grenade towards the van. Within seconds, there was a huge explosion, followed by screams of pain.

With just one grenade Hot-Rod took out four of the guys that came with Manny as well as the van that they came in. Ericka was nowhere to be seen while Manny and Lee were right up front. High-Top could see the two of them creeping closer to them, but he just couldn't get a clear shot at them.

Hot-Rod realized that he had made a mistake, but it was too late now. The only choice he had was to shoot his way out of this shit. As he pulled two sub-machine guns out of his bag of tricks he could see Lee sneaking up on the right of them. Hot-Rod squeezed the triggers and watched as Lee's body exploded from the hollow point bullets that tore into his chest.

As Hot-Rod looked towards High-Top to brag about his kill, he noticed that his partner in crime was no longer moving. Hot-Rod turned just in time to see Manny coming up on him. Before Manny could find some cover, Hot-Rod unloaded on him. As the body hit the ground, Hot-Rod had reloaded and ran over to look into Manny's face.

Manny looked up at Hot-Rod with blood flowing out of his mouth. "Fuck you, you bitch-ass nigga."

That's all Hot-Rod needed to hear. Already full of rage he aimed at Manny and fired another full clip into him. The once quiet neighborhood, now sounded like a war zone. Hot-Rod could hear the sirens getting closer, but for some reason he was frozen in place. He had finally let his anger get the best of him. Now as a result, High-Top was dead. He wanted to run, but the fire inside of him was burning so hot that he couldn't contain it any longer.

Hot-Rod began to walk towards Ericka's house, there was no sign of anyone alive, but he didn't see Ericka anywhere. Not wanting to face the police, he decided to return to his car and get the fuck out of Dodge. As soon as he closed the door and started the engine, he could see the lights from the police cars a few blocks down the road. He pulled off without turning on his lights and made the first right he could.

Hot-Rod wanted to take High-Top's body with him but he knew the best thing to do was leave as fast as possible. He had no clue how he was going to explain what happened, and part of him didn't really care. He knew I would be upset, but at the same time I if no one else would at least understand the anger that Hot-Rod was feeling.

"How the hell did I let that bitch get away?" Hot-Rod said in a mumble. He was more upset about the death of his friend High-Top. Hot-Rod had made up his mind that he was going to avenge the death of his friend, and he didn't care if he had to take on this task alone.

Hot-Rod had a bad night but he had no clue that two more of his friends had also lost their lives that very same night. He drove as carefully as possible, constantly paying attention to the traffic around him. His next thought was, "I need to get in touch with Dre." Hot-Rod knew something wasn't right about the way things went tonight. For some reason he couldn't help but wonder how Ericka got help so fast. It was almost as if she knew they were coming.

When Hot-Rod finally made it home, two of his workers were there waiting on him. Before he could even get out of the car, DJ, the older of the two, walked up to the car. "Someone set Dre up."

Hot-Rod looked at him as he exited the car. "What the fuck are you talking about?"

Justin, the second worker, angrily said, "Tank and Mike got killed. Dre said that they were waiting on them when they got there."

DJ continued, "Gino called and told us to meet you and High-Top here. Where is he?"

Hot-Rod was more upset now than he was at first. After what he just heard, it was beginning to make sense. Somehow, Ericka had known everything that we planned. But the only way that could be possible was if someone in the crew told her. Now there was a new problem. "Who the fuck is responsible for this shit?" Hot-Rod mumbled.

DJ and Justin had no idea what he was talking about. Seeing the anger in his eyes, neither of them said anything else about High-Top. They knew something bad had happened, but they didn't want to push Hot-Rod and make him explode.

Hot-Rod didn't bother going in his house. He told DJ and Justin to get in the car, and they drove off to meet me.

CHAPTER FOURTEEN

The fucked-up thing was that I lost three of my closest friends. Tough as I like to think I can be, this shit was driving me mad. Part of the thug mentality was to not let anything get to you. Well, it doesn't look like I did a very good job.

The hardest thing I ever had to do was to bury a friend. Damn, and I had to bury three of them within a couple days of each other. Just seeing Mike and Tank lying there in those big-ass caskets seemed to be a dream. And though High-Top wasn't as big, we felt the same pain from losing him.

The police had asked a million questions, trying to get some explanation as to why our friends were at these crime scenes. Everyone played dumb and said nothing. We knew that they would be watching us now, we just didn't give a fuck. We didn't start this shit but we were sure as hell going to finish it.

Reggie had been telling everyone about the feeling that we were being watched. We all trusted his gut, so far it had never lead us the wrong way. Every last member of the crew was getting ready for this fight, even the wannabes. The police may be watching us now but what was the worse that could happen. If they wanted some of this, we would damn sure give it to them.

Besides all the shit that was already going on, after talking to Hot-Rod, we realized that someone in our crew was a snitch. Somehow, we had to find out who it was. The thought of somebody that we knew being a snitch seemed crazy. But there was no other way to explain how Ericka and her crew had known what we planned.

All the top guys in the crew got together so that we could discuss our next move. As close as we were, no one knew who to trust. As hard as it was for me to believe that we had a snitch in our group, I knew there was no way it was one of my top guys.

It was time for a meeting of the minds. We decided to meet at the yard so that we could figure out what to do next. No one had any idea who it was, but we were going to find out. The last thing any crew needed was a snitch. It's even worse when you didn't know who it was.

It was a warm Tuesday morning when we decided to have our meeting. It looked as if we were the mob because of all the cars parked outside the yard that day. Because we still had a war going on, we had a few of the most trusted workers there on lookout.

I knew I could trust the young bucks that I took with me to hit Matt, so I made sure to have them there. D-Dog had his brothers with him, and Dena and Brooklyn had their crew as well. I never liked having a lot of thunder cats around but just having the young bucks with me, made me feel a million times safer.

Normally I would do most of the talking, but it seemed Hot-Rod had the most to get off his chest.

"Everybody shut the fuck up!" he exclaimed. Several of the men laughed, but all complied. "We need to find out who the bitch is, and we need to do it today," he continued.

I think we all could see the pain in his eyes as he spoke in detail about the night we lost our friends.

After several minutes of speaking Hot-Rod asked, "Does anyone have an idea who would betray us like that?"

Even after listening to everything Hot-Rod had to say, no one had a clue.

Lott blurted, "Which one of ya'll been talkin' to

your women? You know if you make your woman mad she'll end up stabbing you in the back."

We continued to talk among ourselves yet we couldn't solve anything. After several hours of talking, we were no closer to finding out who the snitch was than we were when we started. After all the talking we decided to watch everyone a lot closer.

We may not have accomplished what we wanted, but a few of the guys did manage to get a li'l buzz on. It was common for us to drink at our meetings, but this was one time I didn't even think about drinking. Even if the rest of the guys didn't care, I wasn't going to rest until I found out who betrayed us.

As we were all leaving, I pulled Hot-Rod to the side. Even though I was close to all my crew, Hot-Rod was the one I trusted the most. I had an idea and I wanted to see how he felt about it.

"I'm thinking about having a few of the young bucks do a li'l creeping," I told him.

Hot-Rod looked at me, "That might not be a bad idea."

I really didn't expect the response I got from him, but I was pleased to get it. Before I could tell him more about what I was thinking, he said, "Who do you want to use?"

I thought for a moment and answered, "I'm thinking bout using the ones that are here now. After the rest of the guys leave, we'll talk to them."

When the rest of the guys had gone we sat down with all the bucks and had another meeting. Part of me felt bad about doing this behind the others backs but I knew it had to be done. As we talked to them I could see how the idea of moving up in the organization made them happy. As much as I didn't want to believe it, part of me felt that the snitch was closer to the top than I thought.

Everything was in motion and there would be no turning back now. If any of the guys noticed someone following them, they would kill them, no questions asked. This would be one of the most important jobs these young guys had ever done for me, I was just hoping it wouldn't be there last.

As I watched D-Dog, John, and their brothers leave the yard, I knew that they would no longer be young bucks to me; they were now men.

John looked at his brother, Danny. "I told you we would move up."

Danny laughed back at him. "You couldn't tell me shit; I already knew."

Dena and Brooklyn were handling it a lot differently. They left the yard almost in total silence while Austin and Brandon walked and laughed all the way to their cars.

Eight balls of fire being let loose on my crew, and I'm the one that put them there. This could turn out to be a big mistake, but I needed to find out what was going on and who was snitching. If anyone could find the snitch it would have to be these guys.

CHAPTER FIFTEEN

As Gin pulled up to pick up her friend, Nicky, she couldn't help but wonder how things were going for her man. It bothered her knowing that he was out there fighting a war, and he could be killed at any time.

"What's up, girl?" Nicky asked Gin as she climbed into the truck.

Gin looked over from the driver's side at her friend as she seemed to struggle getting in. Gin laughed, "You look like you need a ladder, girl." It was a common joke between the two women. Gin often felt short, standing only at five feet two inches tall, but Nicky was even shorter, and Gin made sure to remind her of this every time they got together.

Gin was going to spend the day with her friend shopping. They hadn't had a chance to go out since all the shit had been going on with Ericka. She was far from scared but knew that it was dangerous for her and anyone that was with her.

The ladies decided to spend their day shopping at union station because they could find anything they needed there. It was one of the biggest and best malls in the city, and there would be less of a chance that something would happen in such a populated area.

Gin headed downtown to the mall and as she was driving she noticed a black Ford Mustang that appeared to be following her.

"Do you see that car behind us?" Gin asked Nicky.

Nicky turned to look and said, "Do you mean the black one?"

Gin smiled. "Yes, the black one. I think they're following us."

Nicky often tried to act tough, but there was no hiding her fear. "What are we going to do? Who do you think it is? Are we going to be all right?"

"Slow down," Gin ordered. "We'll be okay. We're almost at the mall. If I need to I'll call Dre when we get there." Nicky settled down a bit, but the fear was all over her face. Gin began to regret saying anything, but it was too late now.

As Gin pulled into the parking lot at the mall she saw the black Ford pull in on the other side of the lot. She never panicked, and this time was not any different. "Let's go spend some money, girl," she said to her nervous friend.

Nicky slowly exited the truck. "I hope everything's okay."

As they walked across the parking lot towards the mall entrance, Gin looked back to see if her followers were coming.

"What the fuck?" she mumbled.

Almost panicked Nicky asked, "What, is something wrong?"

Gin stopped. "Do you see who that is?"

Nicky had no idea who she was looking, at but she acted as if she did.

Gin yelled out, "What the hell are the two of you doing here?"

"Probably the same thing you are." The young woman laughingly said back to her.

"Shit, I thought you were following me," Gin told her. As the two people stopped Gin introduced them to her friend. "This is Reggie and Holly, and this is my friend, Nicky."

Nicky smiled. "Hello." She recognized Reggie but had never seen Holly.

Gin, now relieved, said to the couple, "So why don't we all hang out together?"

After a brief discussion the group entered the mall never taking notice of the two men that were behind them. These two men had been following Reggie and now they had a better target, they found my wife. Gin was a very cautious person and many had found it hard to get so close to her. Who would have ever thought an accidental meeting would be all it took.

As the four traveled through the mall, in and out of stores, they appeared to not have a worry in the world. Reggie and Holly seemed to really care about each other and Gin enjoyed seeing them happy.

"So what would you say if I told you I was getting married?" Reggie asked Gin.

Jokingly Gin answered, "I hope it's to Holly, since she's the one here with you."

Holly slipped in, "I wouldn't marry him; he's a gangster." They all laughed so loudly that people began to stare.

Gin told the couple, "Congrats. So when are we going to pick out the rings?"

Reggie smiled, "As soon as you can go with me and help me pick out the right one. I want the ring to be a surprise, but I need a woman's taste. If I pick it out alone it might look like this." Reggie put his hand out and showed the ladies a big gold-and-diamond ring.

"Where the hell did you get that?" Nicky asked, with her eyes as big as pool balls.

"Dre got all of us these rings about a year ago. Hell, if you think this is something you should see Gin's."

Nicky was almost embarrassed at the fact that she hadn't noticed the ring on Gin's hand.

Seeing that her friend was suddenly uncomfortable, Gin interrupted. "Well, how about we leave Nicky and Holly here to chat and we go look now?" Reggie agreed, kissed Holly on the cheek, and he and Gin headed to the jeweler's.

As Gin and Reggie disappeared into the crowd at the mall, one of the two men that had been following the group decided it was time to make his move. He walked over to the table that Holly and Nicky were sitting at. "Hello beautiful."

Holly ignored the man's comment but Nicky happily responded. "Well, how are you, good looking?"

Nicky had a boyfriend named Chuck but she was looking to move on. Even though she loved Chuck, he never seemed to be able to make her happy. Whenever she got a chance, she went fishing.

The stranger asked the ladies, "Why are you two fine ladies sitting here alone?"

Nicky looked the man over, taking notice of how well dressed he was, but paying even more attention to the large rings on his fingers. She blushingly said to him, "I'm not alone now that you're here. What's your name?"

He extended his hand to grasp hers. "My name is Milo. And you are?"

"My name is Nicky, and this is Holly, but she's getting married soon, so you're all mine."

Milo knew he was in now. He had no clue it would be so easy. Now all he had to do was find out what this Nicky girl knew. If he played his cards right he might just be able to get him a li'l pussy as well as getting the info he needed.

Rob, Milo's partner sat back and observed from a safe distance. He knew his partner was taking a chance, and he wanted to make sure nothing happened to him. After all, it was Rob that asked if they could do anything to help with the case.

Milo and Rob had been partners for only few months but they really liked working together. Both wanted to be detectives, so the idea of doing detective work made them feel big as life.

After about thirty minutes, Rob noticed Reggie

and Gin returning from their journey. They were laughing and joking until they noticed an unfamiliar man talking to Nicky. Reggie didn't really know Nicky, but the thought of a stranger talking to her seemed to piss him off. Rob could see the anger in Reggie's face but he knew that this was not the time to be seen, it was the time to watch.

Reggie never liked strangers, so he did not hesitate. "Who the fuck are you, and what the fuck do you want?"

Nicky was very fond of her new friend, Milo, so she hurried to his defense saying, "This is my friend, Milo. I know him from my neighborhood."

Gin knew her friend was being deceptive but didn't want to confront her in front of a stranger. Instead she just introduced herself and decided to wait till later. "Hello, my name is Gin," she said to the stranger as she looked at her friend.

Even though she didn't understand why, Nicky could see that Gin was somewhat upset.

As Reggie sat down next to his soon-to-be wife, the feeling of being watched came over him again. He didn't trust this stranger, and he didn't care what Nicky had to say about it. He looked Milo over once or twice. "I know you're a fucking cop, so why don't you just tell me what the fuck you want."

Milo wasn't sure if Reggie really figured him out, but he wasn't going to panic. The best thing for an undercover cop to do was always keep his cool. Milo had to think fast. He looked at Reggie."I ain't no fuckin' cop, man. What the hell makes you think I am?"

As nervous as he was, Milo knew that Reggie was just checking him out.

Reggie thought for a long moment before responding. He knew that this guy didn't seem right; he just didn't know why. "Something's not right about you, motha fucka, so I suggest that you leave," Reggie said. He watched Milo to see how he reacted to what he said.

Milo knew he had to stay calm. The wrong reaction could set Reggie off and that could ruin any chance he had of getting any information. He looked directly into Reggie's face. "Let's start this shit over. Hello, everyone, my name is Milo. I was wondering if this young lady would consider going out with me sometime in the near future."

Nicky blushed, looked into his eyes, and answered. "Of course I would." She really didn't know this guy but she couldn't help wondering if they would hit it off together. She stood. "So when are we going out and where are we going?"

CHAPTER SIXTEEN

"You still fuck with that same bitch?" Alpo asked his partner Bake.

"Wh, wh, wh, why she got, g, g, g, gotta be a bitch?" Bake stuttered.

Alpo didn't really like Bake's girlfriend, Tay, but she made his nigga happy, so he let it be. Alpo was deep in thought about what I had said to him a couple day ago. He had no idea how he was going to tell Bake that I wanted them to move back to York, Pennsylvania, until things cooled down. He knew Bake would want to take Tay with him and nothing he could say or do would change his mind. Alpo took a deep breath. "Well, Dre wants us to pack shit up and head back to PA."

Bake looked at his friend with even more confusion than normal. "S, s, s, s, so wh, wh, what are w, w, w, we going to d, d, d, d, do?"

Bake had already made up in his mind that Tay was going with him. He knew Alpo didn't really like her, but he didn't care what anyone said about it. "Well, I'm taking my girl with me."

Alpo looked at his friend with amazement. "How the hell did you say that without stuttering?" Bake always stuttered, and the fact that he just spoke without any hesitation, let him know that his friend was very serious about what he just said.

"Don't nobody give a fuck if you take yo bitch wit you, nigga; that's yo baggage," Alpo told Bake.

"I t, t, t, told you she ain't no b, b, bitch," Bake responded angrily.

The two men sat in their hotel room quietly for several minutes, before going to get something to eat. They decided to swing by Ayanna's crib while they were out, to see if she wanted to smoke a li'l bit. When they pulled up in front of her house, there was no need to ask her if she wanted to fire up because she was already smoking.

"Damn, girl, is that all you do?" Alpo yelled to Ayanna, as he and Bake pulled up in front of her house.

She laughed and responded loudly, "Till the day I die."

As the two men parked, Bake took notice of Sean

sitting on the porch. He knew that none of my crew liked that nigga and he didn't feel comfortable with him being there. "We chillin w, with that asshole?" Bake asked Alpo.

All Alpo could say was, "That's her man, not mine."

As the two men exited the car Alpo removed a bag of weed from the glove compartment. He looked at Bake. "Let's go smoke some good shit, fool."

Bake laughed and said, "Cool."

"I didn't think ya'll would come by," Ayanna said.

Alpo smiled. "Why the fuck not? I said we would come by and smoke with you today."

Before Ayanna could say anything, Sean stood up. "I'll roll the shit up."

Although Alpo didn't like Sean, he passed him the baggie of weed. "You better roll this shit up right. This ain't no bullshit; it's good shit."

Sean looked at him. "Nigga, I know what I'm doing. I got this."

Bake and Ayanna sat on the porch talking and laughing, while Alpo went inside to use the phone. Ayanna knew that Sean was jealous but she didn't care, as a matter of fact, she liked it. She looked over at him. "Is there a problem?"

He angrily looked at her and said, "We'll talk about it later."

Ayanna had been looking for a way to get Sean fucked up; she was hoping this was her chance. She shouted back at him, "Fuck that. We can talk about it now."

Sean knew he didn't have a choice now, but he worried about how far things would go. He looked straight into her eyes. "I was just wondering, why you always up in some nigga's face?"

That was all it took for shit to get started.

"Motha-fucka, you don't own me. If I want to be in another man's face, I'll do it, and it ain't shit you can do about it," she barked at Sean.

Now looking as if he was going to cry, "But I thought you wanted to be with me."

As Alpo came back out on the porch, he heard what Sean had said and couldn't hold in his laughter. He hadn't really known Sean that well, but this just confirmed what he had already thought, that Sean was a bitch. He looked into this broken man's face. "If you can't stop crying like a li'l bitch, you gotta go."

Sean was furious now. He hated the idea of anyone laughing at him. "Fuck all of ya'll!" Sean exclaimed as he stood up, dropping the weed on the ground. As his blood began to boil he suddenly seemed to be full of courage. He looked at Alpo and

Bake. "I ain't scared of none of you mother fuckers. I'm sick of all ya'll shit."

Bake stood up and without the slightest hint of a stutter, "So what you want to do about it, then?" Bake was never quick to fight, but for some reason, he seemed eager to confront Sean.

Without thinking, Sean blurted out, "I'll take all ya'll down; just wait and see."

Confused Alpo said, "What the fuck you mean by that?"

Ayanna didn't give Sean a chance to answer Alpo's question. She quickly jumped up and punched Sean in the mouth. As she watched the blood flowing from his mouth and nose she told him, "Get the fuck out of here!"

Sean walked off the porch and headed down the street. As he was leaving he looked back and shouted, "That's all right; it ain't over yet."

CHAPTER SEVENTEEN

"So did you hear anything else from Milo?" Goode asked Sellers.

"He got the information we needed so we should be able to make our move soon," Sellers answered.

"Did he find out who was behind this shit?"

Sellers didn't want to answer his partner. "He couldn't find out any names, but he did give me a few locations."

Sellers had found out more than he was willing to let his partner know. Although he was a rookie detective, he had several good informants in the streets. He trusted his people, but they dropped a bombshell on him.

Goode could tell his partner wasn't telling him everything, but he couldn't figure out just what he was hiding. He smiled. "Well, whenever you're ready to make that move, just let me know."

"You can bet I will," Sellers said. As he watched Goode walk away he couldn't help but wonder how his partner got himself caught up in this shit. He knew that most of his fellow officers didn't like his partner, and maybe now he could understand why.

Sellers was angry and confused. He hated the idea of a dirty cop, but the fact that it was his partner made it even worse. And now he had to do something about it.

As Sellers sat wondering what his next move would be, the phone rings. After the third ring.

"Narcotics squad, detective Sellers, how may I help you?" After several minutes, Sellers hung up the phone and rapidly left the office. On the way out he stopped at Milo's office. "I need to talk to you. It's important," Sellers said.

Milo looked up from the papers he was reading. "What's up?"

Sellers hadn't really known Milo that well, but he believed that he could trust him. Several of the officers in the precinct had often spoken of how dedicated Milo was. Sellers figured that if anyone would be willing to help him it would be Milo.

Sellers told Milo, "I know that you got a lot of information from that chick you're fucking, but I found out from some of my people in the streets that Goode is involved."

Milo seemed shocked by what he just heard. He looked at Sellers, "You fuckin' with me, right?" Milo laughed, "I never liked his bitch ass anyway."

Sellers sat down. "We need to catch him in the act. He's not dumb, but he is greedy as hell." After a while, Sellers said, "How about we catch him making a buy."

Milo jumped up. "That might just work. Do you have somebody that can help us?"

"Yeah," Sellers said, "And I might be able to set it up this week."

As a huge smile came over Milo's face. "I've been waiting on a chance to get that fucker."

Sellers looked down as if his feelings were hurt. "You and everybody else."

CHAPTER EIGHTEEN

"Just shut the fuck up talkin' to me!" Lott barked at Niecy.

She loudly responded, "What the fuck you gonna do? Nigga, you just like a Pop-Tart, hard on the edges and soft everywhere else."

Lott knew it was no good arguing with Niecy, and for some reason she seemed to be more upset than usual. He looked at her. "What the fuck is your problem? Why you acting like a bitch?"

Neicy turned to walk out of the room, "I'm tired of all this drug-dealing shit. This is not what I thought my life would be like when we got together."

Lott felt Niecy's pain. He never planned to be in the game so long. Truthfully he planned on getting out years ago. He looked at his woman as she stood in the doorway. "Baby, if you want me to quit, I will. Just say the word."

"That's the problem, I shouldn't have to ask," she said. Neicy turned and left the room.

As she walked away Lott yelled at her, "Well, I shouldn't have to change who I am, either. I thought you loved me for me."

Niecy looked back at him. "And I thought you loved me enough to keep me and my kids safe."

Lott didn't bother to say anything else; he knew she was right. He cared about her, but he loved his lifestyle, and he wasn't going to give up either one until he was ready. "What the fuck am I going to do?" Lott asked himself. Just then the phone rang. He picked up the receiver, "Hello."

"What's up?" the voice on the other end said.

"What's up, Hot-Rod?" Lott said.

"Shit, just tryin' to see if you want to go to the track with me and Dre today," Hot-Rod said.

"You know I do. What time?"

"We'll be there in about thirty minutes. Can you be ready by then?"

Lott paused for a moment. "I'll be ready. I need to get out of here for a while anyway; my woman's acting like a bitch anyway."

After Lott hung up the phone he knew he had to let Niecy know that he was leaving. He hated to leave when they were arguing, but it was always the best thing to do. Maybe if he gave her time alone she would feel differently, or so he thought.

"Niecy!" Lott yelled. He thought she might not answer but he wanted to at least try.

Surprisingly she answered. "What the fuck do you want now?"

Lott quickly responded, "I'm going to the track with Dre and Hot-Rod. Do you need anything before I go?"

He waited for a response but she just turned and walked away without saying anything at all. Lott didn't bother to say anything else. Instead he just remained quiet and got dressed. Sadly, he knew in his heart that things would never be right between him and Niecy again.

After a few minutes Hot-Rod and I pulled up in front of Lott's house to pick him up. I never liked blowing horns; that always seemed to attract too much attention, so we got out of the car and walked to the front door. I knocked on the door and Niecy answered.

"What's up Dre, Hot-Rod?"

I shot her a quick smile. "Not much, sis. Where your man at?"

She raised her finger and pointed to his office.

As Hot-Rod and I walked into Lott's office he was

hanging up the phone. He turned to look at me. "I think I know who the snitch is."

I didn't bother to tell him what the young bucks Paul and Danny told me earlier that day. "Well, who the fuck is it?"

Lott stood up shaking his head. "It's that mother fucker…"

CHAPTER NINETEEN

In a small hotel room downtown, Ericka sat, trying to figure out what her next move was going to be. She never was able to recover after the deaths of her top men, but she didn't give up either. As she stood looking out the window at the river front, there was a knock at the door. She opened the door.

"What the fuck took you so long? You were supposed to be here almost an hour ago."

The hooded young man harshly responded, "Bitch, fuck you. I'm helping you, so chill the fuck out."

Amazed by the aggressiveness of her visitor, she replied, "You must have me fucked up with yo' momma. I don't give a fuck if you're helping me or not. If you ever talk to me like that again, I'll put a bullet in your head. Do you hear that?"

"Whatever you say baby, but you need me if you want to take that mother-fucker Dre down," the young man said to her.

She smiled at him. "I'm glad you think so, but I don't really need you."

The young man was no longer feeling as sure of himself. Not feeling as confident, he asked, "So what do you need me to do?"

She knew she had him; now she was in control. She looked at him. "It's not what I need you to do; it's what you can do for me." She looked to see the confused expression on his face. "Just in case you didn't know, I don't really need you."

The young man was shook now. He didn't know if she was serious or not, but he decided not to take a chance. He sat down. "I can help you set up Dre and his top men, though."

Ericka quickly turned. "Can you get that Arthur guy?"

Puzzled, the young man said, "Do you mean Lott?"

Just the sound of the name made her cringe; she gritted her teeth. "Yes."

He knew he was back in control now. He smiled at her. "Baby, I can get any one of those mother fuckers you want."

Ericka didn't really know Hot-Rod, but she did find out that he was there the night that Manny got killed. She also knew that Hot-Rod was one of my closest friends. She thought if she took him out I would definitely break. "What about Hot-Rod?" she asked softly.

He smiled and said, "I can get him too."

She sat in the chair next to the young man.

"So how exactly can you do that?"

The young man sat and spelled out his plan for taking me down. Ericka listened to everything he had to say without any interruptions at all.

After he finished what he had to say, she looked at him harshly. "If you can make that shit work, I'll give you anything you want. Hell, I might even make you my bottom bitch."

They both laughed for a moment, and before anything else could be said the phone rang. Ericka answered the phone. "Hello." After listening for several minutes, she replied, "Okay, we'll take care of that," and hung up the phone. She looked at the young man. "How fast can you set your plan in motion?"

He smiled. "Right away. Today if you want."

Ericka was somewhat bothered by the phone call, but she didn't think it was a big deal. She had this young man, as well as several others helping her to bring me and my crew down. The fucked-up thing was that no one ever knew that she had an older sister.

A smile came over Ericka's face as she thought about what her caller told her. She knew that things were about to get really crazy, and she welcomed it. "So tell me again what you want from me," she asked of the young man still sitting at the table, enjoying his drink.

He put his glass down. "I'll tell you what. You tell me what you have to offer, and I'll let you know if it's enough."

The young man now had the upper hand. He could see that Ericka had no idea what to say next. Instead of waiting on a response he decided to fuck with her head a li'l bit. With a smirk he said to her, "What would you say if I just wanted you?"

Ericka's chin dropped. She was stunned. She looked at him. "What the fuck do you mean by that?"

The young man laughed. "You can figure it out."

Ericka was somewhat flattered by the young man's request. She had no idea if he was serious or not but, she thought it might just help her get the upper hand. If she could whip it on him real good, she might just be able to keep him in check. As she sat down on the side of the bed she flashed him a flirtatious smile. "How much of me do you want?"

The young man slowly stood and walked over to Ericka. He thought to himself. "Is it really this easy to fuck this hoe?" He had seen Ericka a few years before when he was with me. He remembered just how innocent she looked back then, and thought, *If only she was like that now.*

Ericka sat and wondered why this young man didn't act like he was interested in her. She didn't think she looked that bad. As a matter of fact, she thought she looked fine.

Before she could question him he stood up. "I'm not really sure what I want at this time. When I decide, I'll let you know."

She looked at him and wondered what was really going on in this young man's mind. "I just hope it's not more than I can give you."

"I would never expect you to give me more than I deserved."

The meeting was over, and it was time for the young man to put his plan in action. "I need to get in the streets and get the wheels rolling."

Ericka smiled at the young man and stood to walk him to the door. "Call me and let me know how things are going."

As the two of them made their way to the door Ericka thought for a moment. "You know what? I don't even know your name."

The young man smiled. "My name is..."

CHAPTER TWENTY

Gino sat down with John and Danny. "Shit's getting crazy, man. I want ya'll li'l mother fuckers to be careful out there." After several weeks of violence, Gino was concerned and didn't want anything to happen to his young boys. He lost several of his workers in the last few months, but he had more of a connection with the young bucks than anyone else. Hell, at times he would even tell people that they were his li'l cousins.

"You know we can handle this shit, man," said Danny.

John smiled, like he did all the time. "The problem is, we need to get these bitch niggas out the way."

Almost every time the crew planned to do something there ended up being some kind of problem, either with the police or with Ericka's crew. It was time to buckle down and take care of shit again, but this time only a select few would know the real plan while others would hear a false plan.

D-Dog and Paul finally arrived at Gino's house. They had gone to get something to eat for everybody, but it took longer than they thought it would. Paul walked in. "Man, them mother fuckers were slow as hell."

D-Dog agreed. "I didn't think we would ever get our shit."

Gino looked at D-Dog and laughed. "I don't care how long it took, nigga, just give me my change."

As much fun as the young men were having with Gino, none of them could ever imagine that this would be the last time all of them would ever be together like this again. Things were already bad, but they were going to get a lot worse before it was all over.

John sat, eating and laughing, then out of nowhere, said, "You gotta admit, though, that bitch Ashley is thick."

D-Dog looked at John and laughed. "That bitch Paul is fucking with, May, is kind of hot, too."

Gino didn't want to feel left out. "I don't know. I

hear John is trying to be like Reggie. He went out and found him a gal named Holly."

Danny couldn't contain himself any longer. "Fuck all ya'll. All my bitches are fine."

Paul agreed. "I wouldn't be able to pick just one either."

This was an every week thing for these guys. Every week they would get together and drink while talking about women. All of them considered themselves players, but Danny was a borderline pimp. He had at least fifteen different girls all over the city that paid all of his bills as well as keeping him in the freshest clothes.

Danny stood up and brushed off his fresh, white T. "Well, ya'll niggas can sit here and talk about pussy all day, but I'm going to get some."

John looked at his younger brother. "Hey, dummy. At least pull your shirt down over your gun."

D-Dog interrupted, "I know you're going to get your li'l jr. pimp, Ja'Quel. Tell that nigga he still owe me that money."

Danny looked at his big brother. "I'll tell him, but you know that mother fucker don't like when you send him messages. He always says, if you want something from him, ask for yourself."

Gino knew his young boys loved the ladies, and the ladies loved them, but he often worried about them being set up. "Yo, Danny, watch your back with them bitches, man."

Danny brushed his shoulder off. "As good as my back looks, no problem. If one of my bitches trip, I'll just keep steppin' till I find the next one."

Everyone laughed as Danny walked out of the door.

"That nigga crazy," John said. "He can talk all the shit he wants, but pussy makes his ass act a fool."

Gino smiled. "We all have that problem one time or another."

Gino was right; we all had a li'l bit of crazy in us when it came to our women.

D-Dog stood up. "So what's going on with this war shit, Gino?"

Gino took a swallow of his drink and thought for a moment. "I don't know, but it looks like it might be coming to an end."

Paul jumped up. "How the hell is it almost over? We still have niggas dropping dead left and right. Did I fuckin' miss something?" Paul had lost several of his friends during this war. Not only had his friend Quell, taken three bullets in the chest and died, but his niggas Dae-Dae, and Mikey had got caught up in a shootout with the police and lost. The thing that Paul hated the most was that his friends died trying to help him.

Gino paced back and forth across the room. "I know it doesn't seem like it, but we've accomplished a lot in the last few months. Not only has Ericka lost most of her crew, but we're getting close to finding out who the snitch is."

D-Dog hesitated for a moment before saying, "I know. Dre had us checking shit out, and I can't believe some of the shit we found out."

Gino looked at D-Dog with a puzzled look on his face. "What the hell are you talking about? Dre had you checking what shit out?"

John barked at D-Dog. "Damn nigga. You talk too fuckin' much. Didn't Dre tell you not to say shit?"

Paul suddenly started laughing. "Ya'll both fuckin' stupid. Gino knew about it long before we did."

Gino looked at the young men. "Well, that's almost true. Dre told me the same day he talked to ya'll."

D-Dog realized that he made a mistake by opening his mouth, but he knew Gino would never fuck the crew around. Dre trusted Gino and Hot-Rod with his life; they were like brothers.

Four motorcycles pulled up and parked on the parking pad behind Gino's house. Paul quickly reached for the pistol on his waist. "Who the fuck is that?"

John smiled. "Well, quick draw, that's Dena, Austin, Brooklyn, and Brandon. You need to slow the fuck down before you shoot somebody." He recognized them right away; they went riding together all the time.

D-Dog walked over to Dena. "What's up, beautiful?"

Brooklyn laughed. "You call that beautiful? You need to get your eyes checked."

"Fuck you, Brook." Dena answered back. "Anyway, we came by to touch base with ya'll. We need to get together with Dre and let him know what we found out."

Paul, overhearing the conversation, agreed. "We need to do it fast; I don't think he's going to believe this shit, though."

Gino interrupted. "I'll tell you what; we're all going to see my nigga. I believe everything ya'll said, and he will, too." There was no way Gino was going to miss out on this. These young fuckers found out more than anyone would have ever figured. Paul told Gino about Ericka's sister, the person talking to the cops, and that one of my workers was hooking up with Ericka.

"Well, let's get going," John said. "We need to get this shit out in the open so we can take care of it."

Gino and his young boys had bullshitted around for most of the day. I had taken Gin out for her birthday, and they didn't want to fuck up our day with what they had to say.

Everything was about to go crazy. No one wanted to face the fact that we had a traitor in our crew. It was so much worse to find out that it was someone that we all trusted. As I think back to that day, I can only wonder if things would have been better if we never knew anything.

It was just before midnight when Gino arrived at my house with all the young guns. I opened the front door just as he was preparing to knock. "So what's up?" I asked.

Gino walked in. "We have all the info we need, my nig. It's time to get busy."

This was a good thing. It had been several long months, and we lost a lot of good people. At last we would be able to make someone pay. I looked at Gino. "Did you call Hot-Rod?"

Gino answered, "I thought you might want to hear this shit first."

My mind was racing now. Could my nigga Hot-Rod be behind this shit? "Is he involved?"

John spoke up. "He's not involved; we just know how his temper is. He would fuck around and go on a killing spree."

John was right, and I knew it, but I didn't want to discuss something this big without my best nigga with me. After what we found out from Lott, I was ready for anything. "Well, give him a call and tell him to get here right away. Let him know what's going on."

As I watched the rest of the young guns sitting in my living room, I began to realize that these were the new soldiers in our crew. Even though they had all put in more than enough work, it was time for them to get their own crews. I never thought things would get this bad, and now that they had I couldn't help but wonder if it was all worth it. "Ya'll get something to drink; I'll be right back."

I left the room and went to let Gin know what was going on. As I walked into the bedroom she turned to look at me with the most beautiful eyes.

"Is everything okay?" She already knew the answer to her question.

"No, baby, it's not, but it's getting ready to be."

Now she wanted to know more. "How is that?"

I sat on the bed next to her. "The young guns found out what we needed to know. We're just waiting on Hot-Rod to get here so we can decide what to do next."

Gin looked at me and began to laugh. "Young guns. Just a few weeks ago they were young bucks; I guess they're growing up."

Until that very moment I hadn't realized that I started calling them that. She was right, though; we all changed a lot during the last few months. I just had no clue how much.

After a few minutes, Hot-Rod knocked on my bedroom door. "What's up nigga? I'm here."

I walked to the door and opened it. "I'll be down in a sec."

Hot-Rod knew me well, and he could tell that I was distressed. "All right, bro, I'll see you when you come down."

I gently kissed Gin on the cheek as I watched her nodding off to sleep. "I love you, baby." I turned and left the room, hoping that I would be able to get out of this shit sometime soon.

As I walked down the stairs I could hear the chatter in the living room beginning to quiet down. I walked over to the bar in the corner and made myself a drink. "So who wants to start this shit off?" No one said a thing as I took a swallow of my drink.

Paul and Brandon stood at the same time and said, "I'll start."

It was almost funny for a second, but I quickly motioned for John to start things off.

He looked at me as he began to inform us of what he found out. "Well, I was running with Paul for a while, and we didn't find anything out right away. But when I took my girl out to dinner, I found out who was one of the people talking to the police." I really didn't think he knew what he was talking about, until he said, "I went downtown on the landing, and I saw one of the cops that used to fuck with me all the time. He was walking with..."

CHAPTER TWENTY-ONE

As Sellers pulled up in front of Monroe motel, he thought long and hard about the fact that he was about to take his partner down. He had often heard how other cops looked at snitches among their ranks, and now these very cops would be looking at him the same way. As much as the idea of being an outcast bothered him, the idea of having a crooked partner bothered him even more.

"What the fuck?" Sellers said to himself, as he noticed a familiar face entering the motel room right next to the one Goode would be using soon. Before he could think anything further about it, there was a knock on the passenger-side window.

"What's up, Elvis?" Milo said as he opened the door.

Sellers was nervous as hell about what was about to go down. He looked at Milo as he got into the car and said, "I just hope everything goes down right. I don't want anybody to get hurt."

Milo didn't seem to care at all. "Man, I don't give a fuck what happens as long as we take that fucker down,"

Sellers smiled and looked at Milo. "Why do you hate Goode so much anyway?"

Before Milo could answer the two men noticed Goode driving into the motel parking lot.

"This mother fucker can't show up at work on time but he's early for this shit," Sellers said in a mumble. This was going to be the deepest shit he had ever had to deal with; he only hoped that his nerves could hold up. "Milo, did you take care of getting our backup?"

Milo nodded his head. "Of course I did. Do I look like a fool or something?"

Sellers nervously said, "No, it's not that. I was really just asking to make sure."

It was only seconds before Sellers noticed his informant walking up to the door of room 22, the very room that his partner Goode was waiting in. Sellers figured that they had a great plan; now it was time to get shit rolling. "So how far away is our backup?" Sellers asked Milo.

Milo chuckled and said, "Don't get your panties

in a bunch. They're all around us. As soon as you give us the go we'll be right in."

Sellers checked his wire to make sure it was well hidden, and got out of the car. As he walked to room 22, he had to calm himself down. He stopped in front of the door and turned to look behind him. After seeing that there was no one behind him, he turned and knocked on the door.

"What took you so long?" Goode said as he opened the door. Sellers walked in and closed the door behind him.

As he looked around the room he said, "I had a couple other stops to make on my way here." Goode returned to the table in the corner where a young lady was sitting patiently. Sellers looked at her. "So how are you doing tonight?"

She looked up at him smiling and said, "I'm doing pretty good, but I'm ready to get this shit over with."

This young lady had been an informant for the police for several months now. Sellers thought she was very attractive, but he always had a hard time saying her name, so he often just called her "Beautiful."

He smiled at her and said, "So tell me, Beautiful, what new info do you have for me?"

Sellers had already told Beautiful what he needed her to say, so when she answered him, he was surprised as hell when she said something different.

Beautiful took a drink from the glass she had sitting on the table in front of her, then looked both men over before speaking. "This is really fucked up. I've been helping ya'll for a long time now, and you hung me out to dry." Almost as if she was angry she looked at Sellers. "I know what you told me to say when I talked to you earlier, but you didn't tell me about that other guy."

Sellers looked at Beautiful as if she had pulled a gun on him.

Goode, still sitting across the table from the young lady said, "What the fuck is she talking about, Sellers?"

Before anything else could be said, the room door came flying off if its hinges with a loud boom. Goode and Sellers had no time to react. Milo and his partner, Rob, had the drop on both of them, and there wasn't anything they could do about it.

"Don't do it, Sellers," Rob said as he aimed his shotgun at Sellers' head. A blind man could have seen that Sellers was totally confused; he couldn't believe what was going on. Sellers looked straight into Milo's eyes. "What the fuck are you doing? Was this your plan?"

Milo smiled. "Sellers, you're a good cop, but you need to learn your place."

"That's the mother fucker I was talking about," the young lady said aloud.

Goode slowly stood with his hand up. "I can't believe this shit. Do you think I'm dirty or something, Sellers?"

Sellers felt ashamed about how he had gotten his partner caught up. "Goode, I'm sorry. But all the evidence pointed to you being dirty. Even my people on the streets said you were dirty."

Goode felt betrayed, but part of him understood why Sellers thought what he did.

Goode and Milo began to laugh loudly.

Sellers was now more confused than ever, thinking to himself that this must all be some kind of joke or something. "What the fuck is so funny?"

Goode lowered his hands and walked over next to Milo. "Sellers, not only are you a good cop, you're a smart cop. But did you really think you would be able to set me up?"

Rob looked at Beautiful and asked her, "So do you have anything you want to say?"

She glared at him and said, "First of all my name ain't Beautiful; it's Ayanna. Second of all, fuck ya'll mother fuckers, you just going to..."

That was the last thing she would ever say, as Milo fired two shots into her and watched her body go limp and drop to the floor.

Sellers took a deep breath but didn't make a sound. He knew what these men had planned for him, and he wasn't going to give them the satisfaction of seeing him squirm.

Milo looked at Sellers and tossed his pistol on the floor. "Damn, Sellers, why the fuck did you shoot that fine piece of ass? You should have at least got some first."

Goode smiled and walked towards the busted door. Just as he stuck his head outside to see if anyone was trying to be nosey, Sellers decided to take a chance. As Sellers drew his pistol, he dove into the bathroom and fired two shots at Rob. Much to his surprise, his aim wasn't as bad as he thought it was. Both shots hit Rob center mass and dropped him.

Milo had grown over confident during this whole ordeal, so he didn't even have his pistol drawn. Rather than shooting back, he just dove like a li'l bitch for cover.

Goode on the other hand, was fired up. He fired an entire clip into the bathroom while yelling at Sellers, telling him to bring his ass out. "You know you fucked up now. And to think I thought about letting you live."

Sellers looked down at his leg and realized that one of Goode's shots had hit him. He knew that if he was going to survive, he would have to fight his way out, but how? As he sat there trying to plan his assault, he heard several shots come from the other room.

Sellers reloaded his pistol and yelled, "I'm going to take you down, Goode, and you know it."

A woman's voice called to Sellers, "If you're talking about this fucker here, come and get him."

Sellers did everything he could to find out who this was. He yelled back at her, "Who the fuck are you?"

"Right now, I would say I was your savior," the woman answered.

For a moment, all Sellers could hear was a conversation between this woman and another person. Suddenly Goode yelled out in pain. If Sellers knew nothing else he knew what pain sounded like. "What do you want?" Sellers asked.

A mans voice rumbled through the room. "Officer, if you want this man alive, come out and get him. We're not here for you, but if you come out here the wrong way, we will kill you, too."

Sellers at that time decided to take the biggest chance of his life. "Okay, okay, okay. I'm coming out. Don't shoot."

As Sellers eased out of the bathroom he saw a dark-skinned young man with dreads standing over Goode with a gold-plated AK-47, and beside him was a tall, red-boned girl in her early twenties holding two chrome .38s in her hand. Sellers wasn't sure what was going on, but he was sure that these two weren't there for him.

The young man looked at the woman standing next to him and said, "Baby, looks like we saved a fuckin' pig tonight."

"What's your name, pig?" the young lady asked.

Sellers paused for a second, and looked at Goode laying on the floor. "My name is Sellers, Detective Dustin Sellers."

Goode was in a lot of pain, and judging from all the blood coming from Milo's head and face, Sellers figured he was dead. "So why are you two here?"

The young woman laughed. "Well, Mr. Officer, that's not important. It looks like you or your friends already took care of our problem."

The young man simply smiled. "Let's just say you did us a favor, so we did you a favor."

These two young fuckers actually saved Sellers'

life. For the first time in his career, Sellers finally understood why so many cops end up with thugs for friends."You know I can't just let you walk out of here?" Sellers asked.

The young man laughed. "Motha fucka, I'm Bliss. If you want me, come and get me."

The two young people turned to leave. Sellers thought long and hard for a minute as he watched these two walk away from him. He knew deep inside that there was no way he would be able to take them in; truth was, he didn't want to, either.

The young man walked to the pay phone near the entrance of the motel and made a call. "Yo, Dre, it's done. The fuckin' cops had it done before we even got there."

I was happy that Bliss and Jane came back in town to help me take care of a few things, but I hated the fact that they had to take out other members of my crew. I took a deep breath and said, "So which one do you want to take care of next?"

I knew that at least three more people were going to die in the next couple of days; I also knew that each of the three were friends. The hardest thing was trying to decide who would die next. "Take out her sister."

Bliss was quiet for several seconds; then he said, "What about her man?"

He was my friend, but if he got in the way he would have to die as well. "Use your best judgment. I trust you."

CHAPTER TWENTY-TWO

Bliss and Jane were going to make another hit and I had to be there. One of my closest friends had done me wrong and I just had to know why. I don't think I will ever be able to forget that day. It was a Wednesday morning and I called Bliss to find out around what time he wanted to make his move.

"What's up, B?" I said. I think he was a bit surprised to be hearing from me.

"Shit, just chillin'," he answered in a sleepy voice.

We talked for about fifteen minutes plotting and planning. For this hit everything had to be just right. Now that I was going with Bliss and Jane, we decided to do this shit earlier than originally planned.

I looked at my watch and said, "I'll be there in a second. Let's just get this shit done and over with."

Bliss thought it would be best to take Hot-Rod with us, so I swung by and picked him up.

As Hot-Rod came out of his front door he stopped and picked the newspaper up off his front steps, and a smile came across his face as he read the front of it. As he opened the passenger-side door he said, "They made the front page," and he held the paper out for me to see.

Bloody Shootout Leaves Three Dead and Two Injured at the Monroe Motel

I quickly looked over the article just to see if they had any witnesses. I was surprised to read that a young detective had been found alive and said that there was no one else involved in the shootout.

"Why the hell do you think he said that?"

Hot-Rod started laughing. "Didn't Bliss tell you? They saved that fucker's life."

I looked at him. "You have got to be bullshittin' me."

Hot-Rod continued, "Well, from what I understand, his so-called fellow officers were trying to kill him. Jane shot that mother-fucker Goode just as he was about to shoot him." Hot-Rod may have been laughing, but there was no hint of a smile when he said, "I really hate to do this. They're supposed to be our friends." I could see the anger as well as the pain written all over his face.

I glanced at him. "It's fucked up, but it has to be done."

He looked out the window and said, "I know it does, but that doesn't make it any easier."

Just as we pulled up and parked in front of L.W. Hadley's Roofing company, I noticed Bliss getting out of a black Jeep Cherokee. As he walked towards us I lowered my window. "We're ready."

Bliss walked up to the car. "Are you sure you want to do this? He's your friend, not mine."

I looked up at him and said, "I have to do it, because he's my friend."

Bliss turned, went back to his truck, and we were on our way. Hot-Rod and I said nothing till just before we made it to our destination. He looked at me with a stone look on his face. "Let me kill this bitch. Let me get even for High-Top."

I simply nodded my head in agreement. I knew how he felt; that's the reason Bliss and I had decided to bring him with us.

Bliss parked in front of the house while Hot-Rod and I parked out back on the parking pad. As we got out of the car and walked to the house, I pulled out my pistol and cocked it. Jane and Bliss may have been there to do the job, but this was personal, something I just had to do. I reached in my pocket and pulled out a key. "I never even used this thing."

Hot-Rod sighed and said, "I know, bro. I never used the one they gave me either." This was family, and we were about to have a family feud. I stuck the key in the lock and paused for a moment. I looked at Bliss. "This is it."

I unlocked the door and slowly opened it. As we all entered the house I could feel the tension building inside of me. I was a drug dealer and a killer, but this time I had to take out family, including kids. Bliss, Hot-Rod, and I quietly walked to the master bedroom, while Jane went to the kids' room.

As I eased the bedroom door open I could see them peacefully sleeping. We walked into the room with our guns drawn. There's no turning back now. Suddenly he opened his eyes.

"What the fuck is this, Dre?"

As he said this Niecy jumped up and began to scream.

My pain suddenly turned to anger. "Why the fuck didn't you tell me, Lott? Why didn't you tell me that Niecy was Ericka's sister?"

BRAVO "DRE" MARENTZ

Lott had a look of confusion on his face. He looked me in my eyes, and said, "I didn't know!" He angrily looked at her and continued to talk to me. "Dre, if I had known I would have killed her myself."

Niecy's screams had turned to a hard, silent cry. She looked at the men in her bedroom. "Fuck all of ya'll. I wasn't going to let you mother fuckers take my sister out."

Lott quickly slapped her in her mouth. "Bitch, shut the fuck up before I kill you myself."

Bliss whispered in my ear. "I don't think we should kill him. We should let him kill her and the kids."

Bliss had a good idea. If we had Lott do the killing, at least the blood would be on his hands. I could see the pain and anger in Lott's face. I cautiously took another pistol out of my waistband and handed it to him. "You take care of this shit."

Lott didn't hesitate at all. Niecy didn't even have a chance to scream as Lott turned fired two bullets into her head. All of us were surprised as hell at how easy it was for Lott to kill his girlfriend. Even more surprising was how eager he was to go and kill her kids.

"Let me finish this," he said to me.

I raised my hand and pointed to the door. As he

170

walked in the kids' room, he didn't seem to care at all as he drew down on them and fired two shots into both of them. Lott looked at me and said, "Do you believe me now? Is it over?"

I thought for a moment then said, "Yes, this is over. Now we need to take care of the rest of this shit."

Lott agreed. "I want to go with you, but let me clean this up first."

I said, "Bliss, you and Jane help Lott clean this up. Hot-Rod and I will go and get the other guys together."

We were going to finish this shit. I was tired of all the bullshit, all the games. I was tired of the war. As Hot-Rod and I were leaving, I heard Lott telling Bliss that the gasoline was in the garage. Shit was getting ready to get hot at Lott's house, but things were going to be even hotter in the streets.

I looked at Hot-Rod. "Let's go, bro." It was time to finish this shit once and for all.

Hot-Rod smiled and asked, "Who do you want to take with us?" I really didn't know what to say; after what I just went through I didn't know who to trust anymore.

CHAPTER TWENTY-THREE

Four a.m. on a Sunday morning. This was it, Ericka goes down today. I had all my soldiers meet me at the yard for what could be our last big battle. The young guns were their as well as Reggie, Gino, and a few of Gino's workers D.J. and Justin.

Hot-Rod lit up a cigarette and said, "Yo, bro, we need to get going, it's getting late. We need to at least beat the sun up."

He was right; I just wasn't sure if this was what I really wanted. I looked at all my soldiers there with me, some young in the game, and some veterans. "I want everybody to be careful. We don't know what this bitch has in store for us, and I want us all to make it home safely."

Before we could all leave the yard and get in our cars, Bliss, Jane, and Lott pulled up. Bliss slowly lowered the driver side window and asked, "How long before you're ready?"

"We're ready to go now," I answered. As I got into my car, I couldn't help but wonder just how this shit was going to end. We were on our way to Ericka's hideout, a small warehouse on the south side of town.

Jacquan, one of my newest workers, had been watching the warehouse for a couple of days now. He told me that she had a couple of friends staying with her, but he didn't know who they were. I wasn't surprised, and I wasn't upset with him, he was a new guy. The one thing that did bother me though, was the fact that Jacquan had seen at least fifteen of Ericka's workers there with her.

As we headed south on Grand Ave., I noticed how empty the city seemed this time of day. We appeared to be the only people out and about, as we drove toward a war zone. Ericka had put my crew through hell and still I had no idea why. Today this bitch was going to pay for every drop of blood that my crew had spilled, and I didn't care who else had to go with her.

What some of the other guys didn't know was that someone we considered a brother, was there with Ericka. When Jacquan described the two people that were with Ericka, I knew right away who it was, I just couldn't believe it. How could this mother fucker do this to me, betray me like this? I pulled out a Port and fired it up. After I took a couple of hits off of it, I glanced over at Hot-Rod.

"We need to check everybody out after we take care of Ericka."

Hot-Rod knew exactly what I was talking about. Over the last few weeks, we had found out about not just one snitch, but several snitches. This couldn't happen again; everyone would be suspect from this point on. He looked at me, and nodded in agreement. "At least we know we can trust each other."

As we pulled up in front of the warehouse, it looked like a scene out of a movie. It seemed as if every car door opened at the exact same time. I was going to try a sneak attack, but the anger inside of me wouldn't let me think straight. I wanted to go straight in the front door and nobody was going to talk me out of it. Bliss barked at me.

"Nigga, this is fuckin' insane. We need to be careful."

I angrily said, "Fuck that; this bitch has some talking to do. Now that I think about it, so does that snitch motha fucka inside."

As long as I had been in the game, I knew what the two most important rules were. Always keep your emotions under control, and always pay attention to your surroundings. Today I wasn't doing anything right. As eager as I was to take Ericka out, I should have at least been paying attention to who was following me. I wasn't.

D.J. and his friend Tina were the first to make entry. I couldn't believe how easy it was for us to make our entry. It was really just a plain warehouse with three rooms in the back of it. We eased our way back toward the three rooms, we had enough soldiers with us to handle anything. So I thought.

"Oh, shit!" Hot-Rod yelled, as shots began to ring out from behind us. As we all dove for cover, I saw Ericka and her friends coming out. That's who I wanted. I had to get this bitch. Even with all the gunfire going on I could still hear D.J. yelling, "They shot Tina. They shot my bitch."

There were bodies dropping everywhere around us, but I didn't give a fuck. I had to get to Ericka. I shouted to Hot-Rod, "There that bitch is. Cover me."

Hot-Rod had just as much hatred for Ericka as I did. He fired several shots towards her as she tried to run back into the room she had just come out of.

"Ericka, I'm coming for you, bitch!" I yelled. I

knew she heard me, it was almost as if she was begging me to come and get her.

Hot-Rod ran to me. "Let's go and get that bitch, nigga."

We ran towards the door that Ericka went through while our crew continued to battle with the rest of Ericka's crew. As we tried to enter the room someone inside fired several shots at us. As I reloaded my pistols, I looked at Hot-Rod. "This is it, bro. If I don't make it tell Gin I love her."

Hot-Rod smiled at me. "Nigga, ain't no way you're not going to make it. I got yo back."

He was telling the truth; he would fight with me till the end, and I knew it.

"Let's go!" I said as we made our charge into the room after Ericka. We both ran in blasting, but for nothing; there was no one there.

Hot-Rod looked around. "What the fuck? Where did they go?"

I was just as confused. There were no doors or windows in the room, but they had to get out somehow. As we continued to search the room Hot -Rod noticed something on the floor. "Check this out, Dre," Hot-Rod said.

As I looked at what he was pointing at, I noticed what appeared to be a trapdoor in the floor partially covered by a small throw rug. "This has to be how they got out."

"What do you mean, 'they'?" Hot-Rod asked.

I looked at him and said, "Ericka and the snitch."

Hot-Rod appeared angry. "Well, let's go get the fuckers."

As I eased the trapdoor open, Hot-Rod prepared to fire just in case. Nothing happened, but we could see a small bit of light coming from what looked like a tunnel. Hot-Rod and I eased down the steps into the tunnel; we had no clue which way to go, since the tunnel led two different directions.

"Hot-Rod, you go right I'll go left."

As I cautiously made my way down the tunnel, I could see Hot-Rod slowly disappearing in the other direction. I took notice of the odor and couldn't help thinking that it smelled like an old tavern. I could see something further down the tunnel in front of me moving. It was her, and that bitch didn't even see me coming for her. As I picked up my pace I could see her getting closer. Suddenly I was running after her, and within seconds I was right on top of her. I yelled at her, "Ericka, stop right there."

Hot-Rod had caught up to the snitch, and was dealing with him at the other end of the tunnel. "If you move one more inch, I'll blow your fuckin' head off. Get down now."

As the snitch and his girlfriend got down on their knees, Hot-Rod held in his anger long enough to find out why. He walked around in front of the pair and looked in their faces. He angrily looked at the young man on his knees. "How could you do this to us? We were supposed to be family."

"You called me family, but all of ya'll treated me like shit," the young man said.

Hot-Rod was amazed and confused at the same time.

"What the fuck happened to your stutter, Bake?"

Bake looked up at Hot-Rod. "Mother fucker, I don't stutter for real. I can talk just as good as you can."

Hot-Rod no longer cared about the stutter, he looked down at Bake. "Is this your bitch, Tay?"

For the first time, Bake could feel the anger coming from Hot-Rod. He looked at the young lady sobbing beside him, as if he knew this would be the end. He forced a smile. "Shantae, I lo..."

BANG! BANG! Shots rang out. Hot-Rod wasn't going to give Bake the chance to say goodbye. Tay's body dropped to the floor in a bloody heap of dead flesh.

Bake screamed out in anger, "Mother fucker, I'll kill y..."

BANG! BANG! Again Hot-Rod didn't let Bake finish what he was saying. He stood over Bake and fired several shots into him.

"Bitch, I said stop!" I yelled at Ericka as she reached a door at the end of the tunnel.

She stopped and turned to face me. "Why, Dre? Why did it come to this?"

All I could think was, *How the hell can she be asking me this shit?*

"Ericka, you started this shit. You were supposed to be a friend."

Ericka looked at me with the saddest eyes. "If I was your friend why didn't you look out for me?"

Even as a young dealer, I did my best to always look out for those I knew. I did my best to look out for Ericka, so I had know idea what she was talking about. "I did look out for you, Ericka. What the fuck are you talking about?"

Ericka looked at me with tears in her eyes. "Well, why the hell didn't you help me when that fucker raped me? You helped everybody else, but not me. You didn't even come and check on me while I was in the hospital."

"I never knew you were raped. Who did it?" I asked.

Now with tears streaming down her face, she

looked up at me. "Your friend did it. That mother-fucker Lott raped me when I was..."

Shots suddenly rang out from behind me. It felt as if my back was on fire as I fell to the ground. I could see Ericka's body lying on the floor just in front of me. I looked behind me and saw Lott standing there with a big grin on his face.

"Wow. I never thought that bitch would say anything. Hell, she never told her sister, and I was fucking her."

I looked at him and asked, "So you knew the whole time that Niecy was Ericka's sister?"

Lott laughed as he answered, "Of course I knew."

I didn't know what else to say but, "Why?"

Lott stood there scratching his head like he always did. "I think y'all li'l niggas forgot that I was here before ya'll was even thought of. You came in taking over what was supposed to be mine. Now it will be." Lott raised his pistol and aimed it at my head, but before he could pull the trigger, my nigga saved the day.

Gunfire never sounded so good to me as it did at that moment. As Lott spun around and fell to the ground in front of me, I saw the best-looking nigga in the world.

"I told you I had your back, nigga," Hot-Rod said

with a li'l laugh. As he helped me up he said, "Now, let's get you out of here and get you fixed up."

There was no way I would have made it if it wasn't for Hot-Rod. I was in so much pain he damn near had to carry me. As Hot-Rod and I made our way through the warehouse, I could see that several members of our gang had been injured, but there was no one of Ericka's crew left alive.

As we made our way to my car, I told Hot-Rod, "I need to drive, just in case. You take the other car."

We headed north on Grand Ave. back towards home and the hospital. I could feel the life oozing out of my body. Somehow I lost sight of Hot-Rod, but I did notice the police speeding up behind me. I knew this could happen, with all that gunfire in an area like that. For the first time I didn't have a backup plan, and as far as I was concerned I didn't need one. I didn't speed off, as a matter of fact, I didn't even make it to the speed limit.

As I slowly drove, I reached over and picked up my CD case and thumbed through it. I pulled out a Lyfe CD and put it in. Lyfe. What kind of fucked-up name is that for a man to have? I may not like his name, but his music really hits home for me. As I sit here listening to his music, I couldn't help but wonder how I got here.

I looked ahead of me and noticed a roadblock in front of me. I was feeling weak, damn near dead. I didn't care, though; this was it. I was ready for the end. I stopped just a few yards before the roadblock and fired up another port, and looked down at my pistol sitting next to me in the passenger seat. My whole life was a struggle, and this wasn't any different. I reached out for my pistol and felt the cold, blue steel in my hand. I was surrounded now. This was it, my last stand. As I reached to open my door, I could feel the pain tearing through my body. The door opened...

TO BE CONTINUED...

Lightning Source UK Ltd.
Milton Keynes UK
UKOW041135041212

203158UK00001B/58/P

9 781606 102091